Yeah, Ben

Two Brothers and an Impossible Dream

Larry W. Plummer

Black Rose Writing | Texas

ISBN: 978-1-68433-377-6
PUBLISHED BY BLACK ROSE WRITING
www.blackrosewriting.com

Printed in the United States of America
Suggested Retail Price (SRP) $16.95

Yeah, Ben is printed in Chaparral Pro

*As a planet-friendly publisher, Black Rose Writing does its best to eliminate unnecessary waste to reduce paper usage and energy costs, while never compromising the reading experience. As a result, the final word count vs. page count may not meet common expectations.

To all those who read my first novel, "He Never Forgot How to Love" and encouraged me to write another. I will keep writing as long as I continue to touch your hearts.

Yeah, Ben

Chapter 1

Detective Mitchell slapped the file hard on the table with ominous judgement. He planted his fists on the table, trying to appear ferocious, and glared at the suspect's glazed eyes. "What is your name?"

"I am My Brother's Keeper," was all that was answered.

"That's cute," Mitchell chided. "but it won't be so funny when you're sitting on death row."

"When?" the suspect scoffed. "I've been sitting on death row for a long time."

There was no cockiness or arrogance in that declaration. The suspect was just – adamant and certain.

Mitchell loomed closer, and the young man in chains could smell the garlic on his breath. "Alright, smart-ass, listen…" Mitchell threatened. "The State of Texas leads the nation in the number of death row inmates – and – in executions."

The suspect's ears were covered with months of untamed hair, but he was listening. His mouth was hidden by a beard that had gone wild. His eyes were barely detectable behind squinted eyelids, but they stared back into the detective's eyes. Friend or foe, this young man always looked another man in the eye.

"We have witnesses that put you at the murder scene," Mitchell boasted. "They all picked you out of the line-up."

The suspect's nod showed no concern and no denial. He wasn't going to fight what he knew would be his fate. It just didn't matter.

"We haven't found your fingerprints in our database – yet," Mitchell qualified. "but we'll find out who you are. You may as well tell us now."

There was no change in the nameless man's demeanor, and there was no discernible emotion. He simply lowered his head in submission to the way things were.

Mitchell surmised that this muddled and possibly deranged suspect was not going to be shaken by threats. A new approach was called for. He paced around the room in slow, deliberate steps and stood behind the shackled young man. He now spoke in a softer tone. "This guy you killed – what did he do to you to make you want to kill him?"

"I never wanted to kill anyone," was the only response from the broken young man.

Mitchell was sure he had taken the first step toward a confession. He would continue the path of coaxing an indication of motive. He reached around the bowed head and sunken shoulders and slid the photograph of the murder victim onto the table. "What does it take to break a man's neck, Son? How much force, how much hate?"

The drained young man looked at the picture with exhausted eyes. "I hate no man, and I am not your son."

"No, you're not," Mitchell conceded. "What is your father's name?"

"Daddy!" the boyish voice affectionately proclaimed.

Mitchell was slow to realize or refused to believe that he was operating out of his league. He pushed for just one more piece of information. "If you are your brother's keeper, you must know your brother's name."

The table began to rumble and walk forward, as the chains rattled against it. Mitchell had no idea of the storm he had unleashed. The stout, young bull-of-a-man stood and sent the table splintering against the wall.

"WHERE ARE YOU, BROTHER? WHERE HAVE YOU RUN OFF TOO?"

Mitchell's hand only briefly touched the shoulder of the raging bull. An elbow to the gut doubled Mitchell over. A relentless grip on his throat cut off his air. An unstoppable tug on his hair sent him crashing into the wall that had shattered the table.

Three officers stormed into the room. One hit the seething madman high, and another hit him low. The third pinned him on the floor, and the writhing brother screamed, "I TOLD YOU TO STAY IN THE TRUCK!"

Chapter 2

The officers lifted the 195 pounds of grit and gristle to his feet. They herded him down the corridor toward his cell, and the shackles on the accused's ankles made him stumble.

The desperate young man struggled to plant his feet into his fighting stance and thrashed against the chains. But the officers tightened their grip and pushed harder to keep him off balance.

The frenzied detainee had no wish to do harm to anyone, and he wasn't fighting for his freedom. He was flailing against his bondage only, so he could find his brother.

A petite but brazen young woman boldly stepped in front of the parade and brought it to a halt. She looked at all that hair and all that grit and gristle. She looked at the passion in those fiery eyes with the unexplainable love a young girl has for her first puppy.

Her penetrating eyes burned into the soul of the prisoner, and his knees went limp. He had seen eyes like those only in his Momma's smile, and they were the only eyes that could still his heart.

"You need to step out of the way, Miss," the officer directed. The fearless young woman stood her ground.

The officers side-stepped, attempting to go around, but the feisty female matched their move and kept herself in front of those fiery eyes. "My name is Sarah. What's yours?"

The captive soul melted. He almost smiled and answered, "Josh."

"Do you think we could talk later, Josh?"

Josh nodded in anticipation. Sarah smiled in delight and stepped aside. She watched that mysterious, unyielding fighter being towed past her.

Josh made it even harder on the officers to move him along. In a quick and unexpected move, he spun and dropped to his butt. The officers had little choice than to drag him head-first but backward, while Josh took one more look at those beguiling eyes.

Sarah marched right into Detective Mitchell's office. He was still massaging his scalp and checking for missing hair. He was still choking a bit from Josh's grip on his throat.

"What's the story with that young man they're hauling down the hall in chains?" Sarah inquired.

Mitchell sat back in exasperation and dropped his hands in his lap. "Sarah, you can't keep barging in here like this. Even my detectives knock first."

"But this could be the case that gets me out of your hair, Todd," Sarah argued.

Sarah had been barging into Todd Mitchell's office almost daily, in search of a case that would put fire into her dissertation for her PhD in forensic psychology. She had followed some cases as far as Mitchell would allow. Some might have been worthy of Sarah's passion, but none of them had the fire that she saw in Josh's eyes.

"No, Sarah, not this case," Mitchell rebuked. "That young man is too delusional, too dangerous. I don't want this case to turn into an instant insanity plea before we find some more facts to go on."

"What do you know so far, Todd?" Sarah pushed.

"No, Sarah!" Mitchell scolded. "You don't have the experience for this case. We can't even get the guy's name out of him and..."

"His name is Josh," Sarah simply and emphatically shared.

Mitchell's eyes widened. He stood and walked around to pull out a chair and sputtered, "Have a seat, Sarah." He leaned over Sarah's astounding yet unassuming figure and asked, "How did you find that out?"

"I just asked him," Sarah laughed. "Then I asked him if we could talk later, and he said yes. Could you arrange that, Todd?"

Mitchell rubbed his brow and considered his options. "Do you think you could get his last name?"

"I don't know, Todd, but he wants to talk to me. Does he want to talk to you?" Sarah dared.

Mitchell stroked his hair again to see if any more had been uprooted and cleared his gravelly throat. He was not about to surrender any control to this brash, young force of nature, but he recognized the potential of using Sarah's feminine wiles to achieve his goal. "You are not officially on this case, young lady, but I could let you talk to this lunatic a little tomorrow."

Sarah exploded in ecstatic enthusiasm. "Let's go tell Josh!"

"No, Sarah. Let's just…" Mitchell tried to control.

"Just what?" Sarah quarreled. "Let him toss and turn all night, not knowing what tomorrow will bring? He needs hope. I didn't see hope in that man's eyes. I saw only desperation. Let's give him some hope, Todd. Let's let him believe that tomorrow will be better than today. That's the only way he'll be able to talk about yesterday."

There was no other choice for Mitchell. He had no other game plan. He had lost the first battle with Josh, but he had no intention of losing the war. This highly-educated, pain-in-the-ass woman was his best next play. He shared everything he knew about Josh's case. After all, he knew so little.

Sarah listened and made her notes. The more she heard, the more she knew that this would be the focus of all her attention. This was what she had been looking for. It wasn't just a story. It wasn't just a case analysis. She could feel it. This would be the subject of her every waking hour, as long as it took to hear the next chapter.

Mitchell escorted Sarah to Josh's cell and stood back, allowing her to work her womanly charm. Josh was lying on the bunk with his face to the wall. His breathing was imperceptible to the naked eye. There was no visible evidence that he was even alive. Wherever he was in his dark, formidable world, he was inexorably alone.

"Josh?" Sarah almost whispered.

Josh sprang from the bunk at the sound of the voice that had melted his heart, and in one stride, bounded across the cell. He gripped the bars and pressed his forehead against them, trying to get as close as he could to his soul's captor.

"This is Detective Mitchell," Sarah introduced. "He's going to let us talk tomorrow."

Josh's eyes darted from Sarah to Mitchell and back again. He gulped and nodded in hope that this dream was real.

"But first, he wants to see that we're going to get along," Sarah persuaded.

Josh's bobbing head signaled a promise that he would do anything for just one more moment of the comfort he felt in those eyes. Sarah extended her hand in invitation. Josh reached out with his palm up and cradled that delicate hand. Sarah was real now. She wasn't just a dream.

"We're going to share a little at a time," Sarah proposed, "and get to know each other. Would you tell me your last name?"

Josh shot another glance at Detective Mitchell. He remembered having grappled with this officer of the law. He wasn't proud of it and didn't understand why he had done it. All he knew was that he couldn't trust this man.

Sarah reached through the bars and brought Josh's eyes back to hers, with her hands pressed against his cheeks. "Just that one answer will make the detective go away, and tomorrow it will be just you and me."

Josh bowed and wagged his head. As much as he wanted to escape the hell he was living, if only for a minuscule instant, as much as he wanted just a little while with those ever-changing, yet steadfast eyes, Josh could not disclose the name that he had shamed.

"I understand, Josh," Sarah consoled. "It's ok. How about you just tell me how old you are."

"I'm twenty-four," Josh answered with a sheepish smirk. "How about you?"

Sarah wiped a tear from Josh's cheek. "Same here. I'll see you tomorrow, Josh."

Sarah and Detective Mitchell walked away, Mitchell marching forward and Sarah lagging behind, with her head twisting back for a parting glimpse. Josh strained against the bars to watch that long, reddish-brown hair swish back and forth across that dainty behind. He would hold that vision in his mind as the only reason to hope for tomorrow.

Josh sank back into the bunk, but he did not face the wall. He closed his eyes in a small bit of peace. He knew what he was going to dream about, and he couldn't wait to sleep.

Detective Mitchell stopped outside his office and instructed, "You have one shot, little Miss Know-It-All. Get me his last name tomorrow, or I will boot your cute little ass out the door."

Sarah looked up at the face that was at least a foot higher than hers and fiercely challenged, "Do you have a murder weapon?" Sarah prodded.

Mitchell rolled his eyes and looked at the ceiling.

"Do you have any DNA or fingerprint evidence?" Sarah tested.

Mitchell looked at the floor and ground his teeth together.

"I doubt you even have a motive," Sarah goaded further. "The only thing you have is a suspect named Josh."

Few people dared to speak like that to Detective Mitchell, but he realized that Sarah was his best prospect for gaining the information he needed. Mitchell folded his arms across his chest and cocked his head at this brash, young combatant.

"There's a reason Josh doesn't want to tell us his last name yet," Sarah carried on. "And if you betray the trust that young man has offered me, there are a lot of facts that you may never know."

Mitchell was at a loss for words. He shook his head and surrendered to the veracity of this unyielding fighter and closed his office door.

Chapter 3

Sarah was waiting, not-so-patiently in the interrogation room the next day. She involuntarily fluffed her hair and straightened the wrinkles in her clothes. It was an unconscious act when she looked in her mirror to check the gloss on her lips. After all, she was there to employ her professional skills in delving into the thoughts of an accused prisoner. She was there to discern the inner workings of the mind of a young man who just happened to have a gorgeous smile.

She had her list of questions that would hopefully elicit the responses she needed to understand and evaluate her patient's state of mind and discover the facts that had led to his legal predicament. She also had her list of questions that would hopefully answer what was behind the fire in those eyes and the love in that smile.

The officers brought Josh into the room, cuffed and shackled again, and they sat him in the same cold, stiff chair. The room was just as bright and uninviting as before, except Sarah was there. No amount of facial hair could have concealed Josh's smile.

Two officers stood, each in a corner, and folded their hands in front of them. Josh was ever-vigilant of his surroundings and kept the officers ever-present in the corners of his eyes. He hung his head and mumbled, "Sarah, you said just you..."

"This is not going to do," Sarah balked at the officers. "Please take the shackles off and leave the room."

One of the officers tapped on the two-way mirror, and Detective Mitchell entered the room. "The shackles can come off, but the cuffs stay on. And these officers also stay."

Josh slowly rose, and the officers braced themselves. Josh stated his solemn conviction. "Take me back to my cell – please."

"Wait, Josh," Sarah beseeched. "Give Detective Mitchell a chance to think about this." Sarah cocked her head and glared at Mitchell, just as he had done to her.

Mitchell hated to be backed into a corner and would not be caught conceding. "Look," Mitchell ordered in no uncertain terms, "here's what you'll get. The shackles will come off, and these two officers will be posted just outside the door."

Sarah looked at Josh with that hint of a question in her eyes, "Well?"

Josh looked at the two-way mirror and the video cameras. He considered all the badges that had ears. He leaned over the table, and Sarah met him halfway. "They can still hear, Sarah," Josh whispered.

Sarah leaned even closer to Josh and suggested, "Detective Mitchell's office has windows all around, but there are no microphones."

Josh acknowledged his acceptance of Sarah's proposal with a grin and a nod, but Mitchell was not going for it. "Now hold on there, you uppity little bitch..."

Josh spun his head toward Mitchell and warned, "YOU WATCH YOUR MOUTH."

Mitchell broke, like a spring bursting out of a clock. He grabbed Josh by the throat and slammed him against the wall. This was the payback he couldn't resist delivering. "Listen, punk! You're going to rot in that cell."

"That's fine by me," Josh rasped from his constricted throat. "but if you disrespect Sarah again, I will find a way to rip your head off and shit down the hole!"

Mitchell gave Josh a shot to the gut and right-hooked his jaw. "Lock him back up!" he ordered.

Josh was dragged out the door, and Sarah screamed after him, "JOSH!"

Josh flailed and fought with every ounce of strength he had. It was only the chains that contained his rage. "SARAH!"

Mitchell shook the sting out of his fist and bellowed once more at Sarah, "Get out of this police station and STAY OUT!"

Mitchell bounded out the door, and Sarah was left utterly alone, uncontrollably shaking and panting in shock. She sank in the chair and laid her head on the table, trying to slow her breathing and gather her thoughts. She spoke to herself in unrelenting terms. "DON'T GIVE UP GIRL! You're not defeated until you stop fighting. DO SOMETHING!"

Sarah defiantly raised her head and scrutinized her surroundings. She took notice of the video camera that had caught Josh's eye. She fixed on the two-way mirror that Josh could not abide.

She raced around to the other side of the two-way mirror and found the video recorder that had immortalized the cruel treatment of the young man who had offered himself in defense of her honor. With the videotape stuffed in her satchel, she casually strolled out of the police station. She didn't look left or right, and she measured her steps.

She was slight of frame, but not slight of purpose. Her pace quickened when her feet met the asphalt parking lot. That young man, Josh, had laid claim to her heart, and she was not going to allow him to rot in jail. She was going to see him again, and that's all there was to it.

She fumbled the key into the ignition and made the engine roar. The tires screeched as she catapulted out of the parking space. She slammed the brake pedal, shifted into drive and paused to assure herself, "You've got this, girl." With gentle confidence, she applied even, level-headed pressure to the accelerator and headed straight to a lawyer.

Josh laid on his cold, hard bunk, unwilling to eat or sleep. He didn't see the purpose. He had too much thinking to do. He wondered how long it takes for a body to begin to rot. He wondered how long it would take for Sarah to forget him, or had she already? He spoke words that no one would ever hear. "I'm sorry, Daddy. I-I did the best I could. Momma – please don't cry, Momma. Ben – I met this girl, Ben – she, uh – ah, never mind, Ben. I'll see you as soon as I can."

There was no end to Josh's thoughts, but there was a limit to his consciousness. He slept the unrestful repose of a soul wandering between the darkness and the light. Heaven had been within his grasp, but he now teetered between limbo and hell. He slept until the next morning commanded that he return to his hell on earth.

He didn't resist against the morning light, or against the shackles that stung as they were fastened around his bruised ankles. Pain of body and mind was an old acquaintance now, and hope was out of the question.

The officers didn't need to drag him anymore, they needed only to give him a nudge. He shuffled down the hall in a mindless blur and was seated in that same hellish room.

Sarah wasn't there, and so Josh decided he would not be there. He chose to be absent from the world he no longer acknowledged as his own. He kept his eyelids shut against anything that wasn't Sarah and didn't notice the finely dressed man that was waiting to talk to him.

"I'm Phillip McCay," the distinguished-looking figure self-introduced. "I'm your attorney."

Josh raised his eyelids only a slit to allow a fraction of the bright lights to invade the darkness he preferred. "I don't need a lawyer," he politely declined.

"I have been retained by a Miss Sarah Langston," McCay enlightened.

Josh's eyes flew open, and he winced at the piercing light. "How is Sarah?" he begged.

"She's fine Mr. – uh – Josh. She brought me a video of you being assaulted by a police officer. I doubt, however, that we would have any success filing charges, due to the manner in which Ms. Langston obtained the tape."

"I just want to see Sarah," Josh was clear. "Just Sarah."

"That's why I'm here, Josh," Mckay confided. "I have turned the tape over to the Chief of Police, and he will determine what further action will occur. I have also obtained a court order on your behalf. Another detective will be assigned to your case, and you will see Sarah tomorrow. Just Sarah."

Josh wanted to hug Mr. Phillip McCay. But all his chains would allow him to do is emit a breathless cry of "Thank you."

He had all he needed to draw breath for one more day. All anyone needs is to know that tomorrow will be better than today.

Chapter 4

The sun had not yet risen the next morning when the jailer found Josh pacing around his cell. He crissed and crossed, he zigged and zagged, and he walked in delirious circles as he muttered. He was contemplating all the most important questions. "What's your favorite color, Sarah? Do you like James Bond movies? What's your zodiac sign?"

He could not hasten the sun, and he could not bring light into his cell. Only Sarah could do that. But Josh's pace never slowed, and his questions never ceased. Two more hours of countless steps were nothing for a young man whose heart had no place else to go.

Josh caught sight of his officer escort and flagged them in with his arms as if he was late for the most important meeting of his life. He grabbed the bars and assumed a spread-eagle position, ready to be bound and led to Sarah. But Josh was bound only in handcuffs this time, as his custodians asked, "Are we going to have any trouble today?" Josh shook his head in rapid assurance. "Just take me to Sarah."

Josh was taken to a different room than he had seen before. The lights were dimmed to a comfortable level, and the folding chair was padded. There were windows along two walls, and three officers were posted just outside the door. He rested his cuffed hands on the table and reviewed his thoughts. "Don't ask her what her zodiac sign is. That sounds dumb."

Josh stood as Sarah entered the room, and he nodded in slow, adoring respect.

"I'd hug you, Josh," Sarah endeared, "but I don't think I'm allowed. Have a seat, please."

Josh sat in anticipation of Sarah's every move and every word.

Sarah set her bag of groceries on the table. "I had to talk a police officer into going shopping with me, so I could bring this stuff in," Sarah giggled. She laid out cookies and fruit and bottles of water. Then she sat and reached for Josh's hands.

Josh couldn't reach fast enough. He had barely touched the tender understanding of Sarah's fingertips when an officer outside the room tapped on the window. Sarah withdrew her hands and shrugged, "I guess that's against the rules too."

"I just want you to relax, Josh," Sarah comforted. "There are no microphones in here, it's just you and me. We have one hour today, so what do you want to talk about?"

"You," Josh answered without hesitation.

"Well," Sarah grinned. "That shouldn't take long. I'm a forensic psychologist working on my PhD. I'm a city girl, born and raised. I was a high school cheerleader. I was the one they tossed fifteen feet in the air because I was so tiny."

Josh's smile broadened to match his first chuckle he could remember in a long time, and he reached for a piece of fruit.

Sarah took out her pen and pad and asked, "How about you."

Josh stopped chewing and stared at the pad of paper. That first bite of apple was arrested between his teeth, and the sweet juice was suspended in his throat. He had so many thoughts to share with Sarah, but none of them could be shared with the world through Sarah's pen.

"Josh," Sarah put at ease. "They let me come in here to do my job. They want me to learn all I can about you. I want to know everything, but I'll write down only what you want me to hear."

Josh finished his apple, munching as he contemplated. "City girl, huh? I wonder if she has ever had home-made ice cream." He wiped a napkin across his mouth and engaged, "Aren't you going to eat?"

Sarah grabbed a banana. "I'll eat while you talk. Deal?"

Josh pondered what he dared to say next and then took a chance. "I grew up on a farm with my brother."

Sarah had pulled the banana peel down and picked her pen up again. "Ok, would you like to tell me about your brother? Is he older or younger?"

Josh opened a bottle of water and downed half of it in one breath. He exhaled that big breath and sighed, "He was a half-hour younger."

"You're twins!" Sarah delighted. "Wait – Josh – did you say "was?""

Josh pushed the bottle away and rubbed his temples. His eyelids clamped shut in a futile attempt to hold back even a single tear, and Sarah heard that involuntary whisper of a moan.

"Oh, I am so sorry, Josh," Sarah genuinely sniffled in empathy.

Josh and Sarah sat in silence for a full five minutes. Sarah did not need a college degree to see the love that filled the soul of this beautiful young man. And all the questions Josh had prepared to ask Sarah were interrupted by deliciously painful memories he could not escape.

Sarah decided, "That's enough for today. You can tell me more about your brother tomorrow."

"Please don't go," Josh pleaded.

"I'm not going yet," Sarah assured. "We still have to eat all this stuff. But help me out here, Josh. I need them to think that we're making progress."

Josh looked at the guards on the other side of the windows, who were watching their every move.

Sarah grabbed a cookie and took a huge bite. She chewed for a moment and then spewed cookie crumbs across the table with an "Achoo!"

Josh stifled a laugh and took a bite of cookie. "Gesundheit!" Josh blessed, and more crumbs spewed.

Sarah jotted a note on her pad to convince the officers that information was being divulged and said, "Gibberish!"

Josh shoved the rest of his cookie in his mouth and muttered, "Supercali..."

Sarah jotted another note and responded, "Fragilistic..."

The two soul mates leaned in and sang in chorus, "Expialidocious!" And Sarah jotted another note.

They ate it all. They laughed until they cried, and they pulled it off. No one would have believed that there were any secrets or even a thought that was not shared in that joyous interlude. Sarah had a full page of notes when the officers came in to take Josh back to his cell.

Josh was happy as a lark. "Good afternoon, Officers. I'm sorry we didn't save you a cookie." The officers had to hustle to keep up with Josh as he danced to his cell and yelled back, "SEE YOU TOMORROW, SARAH?"

Sarah yelled back, "YOU'VE GOT IT, COWBOY!"

Josh abruptly halted, and the officers strengthened their grip. "Josh, are you ok?"

"She called me..." Josh started and then stopped. Josh and the officers marched on. Josh's words remained only in his mind. "Momma always called Daddy Cowboy." Josh was now desperately in love and didn't even know what her favorite color is.

The new Detective Hallstrom walked in the room and caught Sarah smiling like a cheerleader. He took a moment to bask in that smile, as he leaned against the door to latch it. His laid-back, non-threatening manner was pleasing for Sarah to see. There were no crossed arms, no scowl, and no intimidating glare as she had known with Detective Mitchell. She was happy to warmly welcome, "Good morning Detective...?"

"Hallstrom, Ma'am. I hear that you took lots of notes today. Do you have anything to report, Ms. Langston?"

Sarah swiftly tucked her notepad in her satchel and spoke in her professional tone. "You know that under the court order, all reports will come through Josh's attorney."

Hallstrom allowed the response with earnest intent but raised his eyebrows in curious interest.

Sarah relaxed her professional guard and contributed in cordial serenity. "I can tell you that Josh used to love life, and he loved his brother more than life."

Chapter 5

Each coming day, it appeared as if a new man was occupying Josh's small cell. But it was the same young man who had grown older than his years. He had lived and loved and lost more than some men could bear.

Now, for however brief a time it might last, his burden was lightened by the sweetest person he had ever known. His shoulders seemed broader, and his chin was held higher, lifted to the sound of her voice that lingered in his mind.

"OFFICER! OFFICER!" Josh was yelling as if the toilet was overflowing, and he didn't have a paddle.

The officer ambled over and grinned at the little dance he saw in Josh's feet. "It's been fifteen minutes since the last time you asked what time it is. Don't worry, Josh, I won't let you miss your date with Sarah."

"But – but…" Josh's right hand was clenching the ragged tufts of his facial hair, and his left hand was lifting up the wiry strands of hair on his head. "It's our second date, you know?"

The officer held back an inward chuckle, like a father whose son was asking to borrow the car. "I believe we could arrange a shave and a haircut."

Josh's boyish smile was on full display, as he was ushered into the room. He wanted Sarah to see everything he felt, and he wanted her to know that under different circumstances, he would speak his heart.

It didn't matter that Attorney Phillip McCay was seated next to Sarah. Josh didn't even notice. Sarah's jaw dropped at the sight of Josh's clean-shaven face, and her smile told Josh that he had already spoken his heart.

Josh didn't know what to say, and neither did Sarah, so McCay was the first to utter a word. "I'm here to demand your release, Josh. They can't hold you any longer without filing charges."

Sarah and Josh's hands met in the middle of the table, and for one, brief moment, everything was possible. Maybe dinner, maybe dancing, maybe just a walk in the sunshine. Two hearts hoped for the same thing. It couldn't be defined or confined or measured. Dizziness is what it was. Josh and Sarah were dizzy with hope and expectation.

Detective Hallstrom almost apologetically opened the door and closed it quietly behind him. "You're looking good today, Josh. Are you ready to tell me your last name?"

Josh's grip on Sarah's hand tightened, and Sarah's eyes never left his. McCay intervened with his professional defense. "Josh is the only one who owns his last name. Even so, without charges pending, I must insist that…"

"Excuse me, Counselor," Hallstrom interrupted. "They found fibers matching your client's jacket on the victim's throat."

Josh's grip waned, and Sarah's grip tightened. This was a bombshell to Sarah, but Josh had felt it was coming.

McCay instinctively countered, "That's not conclusive evidence! Those fibers could have come from any number of jackets!"

"But it's enough to file a murder charge," Hallstrom apprised. Hallstrom watched closely, trying to discern any reaction from his suspect.

Josh's head slowly descended in defeat, and he submitted, "That's ok."

"NO! IT'S NOT OK!" Sarah shouted. "They're going to charge you with MURDER, and that's not ok!"

Hallstrom pounced, "Why do you say that's ok, Josh? Are you ready to make a statement? Do you want this to be over?"

"Don't say another word, Josh!" McCay protested.

Josh didn't say another word. He just stared into those longing eyes.

"Detective Hallstrom," McCay asserted. "I will be asking the court for thirty days to prepare my client's case. And I'll be asking the court to allow extended sessions between Miss Langston and my client."

"Of course, you will," Hallstrom yielded. "And that will give me thirty days to build my case against your client."

Hallstrom leaned over the table and offered Josh his assessment. "I don't have a desire to see you suffer. But I have a job to do, and I do my job very well. I have three witnesses who saw you fleeing from the murder scene with what looked like a body wrapped in a blanket over your shoulder. I don't suppose that you are going to tell me whose body that was."

Josh cupped his hands over his face, and his body heaved in silent sobs. He peered through his fingers at Sarah's cringing face.

"You had better start talking to someone," Hallstrom recommended. "I would suggest that you start talking to those eyes you're looking at now."

Hallstrom abruptly left the room, and Josh saw the tears flood Sarah's eyes. He looked away and talked to the wall, unable to watch the terror take over Sarah's face. "You need to walk away now, Sarah. This isn't going to end well, and I don't want you here anymore."

Sarah grabbed Josh by the back of his head and drew their foreheads together in a lock. "I'M NOT LEAVING, JOSH! You're going to tell me about your brother! You're going to tell me about your Mom and Dad! You're going to tell me everything I want to know about you! DO YOU HEAR ME, JOSH?"

Josh looked at the fire and conviction in that deceptively beautiful face. It was the same determination he had seen in his mother's eyes all his life. With her forehead pressed against Josh's, Sarah pushed and tugged to make his head nod, and Josh did not refuse.

McCay deduced that his presence was no longer required, but he gave his parting advice. "Josh, they have very weak evidence against you, but I have none in your favor. I can help you, but only if you talk to Sarah." With that, he left the room and left Josh's fate in Sarah's care.

Sarah intertwined Josh's hair through her fingers and clenched her hands tight. It was just Sarah and Josh now, and Josh didn't know what to say. "I don't – I can't..."

Sarah released one handful of hair to pick up her pen, but she held on to the other handful. "Tell me about your brother." This was not a request. It was a demand from the voice that commanded every fiber of Josh's being.

And so, the story began. Josh spoke openly, unable to defy the resolve in Sarah's eyes, and Sarah penned his words. She scratched feverishly, but she had to pause often to catch a tear before it blotted her notes. Their journey together had just begun, and Sarah was ready for the long haul. Josh's heart was laid bare on that table, the table that was the only thing separating these kindred companions, sharing the pain of intimacy and the comfort of knowing what none other could unravel or comprehend.

Day after day, Sarah listened to what no one else had ever heard. And night after night, with the assistance of a bottle of wine, Sarah wrote. The first night, Sarah wrote her first report to Phillip McCay, Attorney at Law:

September 18, 2001

The subject, Josh, is a twenty-four-year-old male with a strong, medium build and above-average intelligence.

He possesses over-riding protective instincts, stemming from solid family ties, and unwavering loyalty.

He displays no indication of latent hostility or a preponderance toward violence. He has shown a willingness to cooperate, but a reluctance to provide personal information.

It is my opinion that his guarded responses are prompted by a fearless determination to protect his family.

No facts relating to the criminal case under investigation have been disclosed. However, if Josh is excessively pushed to provide answers he is not ready to divulge, it is my opinion that those answers will never be known.

It is my further opinion that Josh is not ready or able to provide meaningful testimony. It will likely take weeks of psychological help and non-threatening guidance to discover Josh's story.

That's all that Sarah shared with Josh's attorney or with anyone, but that's not all she wrote. She uncorked the bottle of wine and began writing the story of Josh and his brother, Ben.

Their story began on the California coast, and Sarah captured all the love that Josh spoke. She crafted each word to convey all the smiles and all the tears that overwhelmed her heart. After the last tissue tumbled into the pile, her pen dropped to the floor. The bottle was empty, the tissues were exhausted, and all that remained were tears cascading over her cheeks.

Chapter 6

Sarah was not the writer of Josh and Ben's story. She was the editor who transformed Josh's words, laughs, tears, and moans into the most beautiful saga she had ever heard. As she succumbed to the persistent pull of sleep, her printer documented all that she would dream about.

Session 1
9:00 am, September 18, 2001

Against all odds, Josh and Ben dipped their toes in the Pacific Ocean.

There was no earthly reason that they should be wading ankle-deep in the tide. They had ignored all probabilities and pushed themselves until they were waist-deep. They had defied the odds and plunged head-first into the surf.

They were twenty-three years old, Josh being a half hour older. Josh was always the first to bring his head above water and look for the radiant face of his twin brother because Momma and Daddy had taught their boy to never leave his brother behind.

Ben shook the salt water from his face, flung his arms out, and took in all the breath he could because the doctors had said that a Down Syndrome child was not likely to live this long. He submerged again just so he could come up and feel that next deep breath. Every breath was special to Ben because Momma and Daddy had taught their boy that he was not a special needs person. He was just plain special.

Both boys felt it. It was always there. They were in a race against time, not knowing how much longer Ben's frail heart would keep beating. But so long as they splashed and laughed, they were ahead of time.

"I'm ready for a nap in the sun, Ben. I'll race you back to the beach."

Ben always won the race. Josh wouldn't have it any other way. Josh put his sunglasses on and sprawled on the beach towel. Ben followed suit and rested his head on the sand.

The boys' semi-truck was parked just up the hill. It was fully loaded, but nothing was perishable. The load could wait while Josh took a nap.

"Josh?"

"Yeah, Ben?"

"Shouldn't we be getting back on the road? We told Momma we would be back every three months for doctor visits."

"Yeah, Ben. They're not expecting us for another two weeks. We'll make it back home in plenty of time. I'm going to take a nap now."

"Ok, Josh."

Josh closed his eyes, but his ears were always open. There was no telling whether sleep would rest his eyes, but his ears would not miss a sound from his brother's lips.

"Josh?"

"Yeah, Ben?"

"We have to make it to Los Angeles, then Phoenix, then Albuquerque, then – uh..."

"Amarillo, Ben."

"Yeah, and then Oklahoma City, then Joplin, then Wichita..."

"We'll make it, Ben. Now let me take a nap."

"Ok, Josh."

"Josh?"

And so it went with Josh and Ben. And Josh wouldn't have it any other way.

It was October, and the evening fog was rolling across the Monterey Peninsula when the boys were back on the road. Ben peered through the fog and worried, "I can't see anything, Josh!"

Josh let the truck slow to a more comfortable speed and lit a cigarette. "We'll be ok, Ben."

Ben rolled down the window and scolded, "Momma and Daddy wouldn't like you smoking, Josh."

Josh took another drag of smoke and exhaled his response. "I wonder who's going to tell them, Ben. Surely not the guy who left the cap off the fuel tank back in Salem."

Ben hid his face behind the map, and a sheepish chuckle could be heard. "No, he's not going to tell them, Josh."

Ben peeked out from behind the map and spotted the highway sign. "It's only twenty miles to Monterey!"

Josh knew why Ben was so excited. Monterey was the most special place in all of Momma and Daddy's stories. Momma and Daddy sang a love song together in the cocktail lounge of the "Lafonda Motel." It wasn't just a love story that happened in Monterey. Josh and Ben's very existence depended on that song.

"I wonder if they have a room available at the "Lafonda," Josh teased.

"Can we afford it?" Ben hoped.

"Sure, we can, Ben. Remember we got that hundred-dollar bonus for getting the load to Salem early? Well – minus the $8.50 for a new fuel cap."

Ben bounced in his seat for the next twenty miles, and Josh switched on the radio for a little bouncing music. Ben bounced higher, and Josh laughed louder. He had too little breath for another drag and flicked the cigarette out the window.

The LaFonda's vacancy sign was lit and invited the boys in. Josh threw his bag on the bed and started to strip his clothes that were stiff from dried salt water.

"I'm ready to go eat, Josh," Ben urged.

"We have to shower first, Ben. We might meet some ladies."

"Ah, Josh," Ben blushed.

Josh was trying to shave in front of the steamy mirror while Ben took his turn in the shower. Ben's voice gurgled under the shower head. "You ever had a girlfriend, Josh?"

Josh reflexed and nicked his chin with the razor. Blood trickled in a scarcely felt but very noticeable stream. "Sure, I have. Remember Angie in high school?"

"Yeah, I remember Angie," Ben thought back. "Did you ever kiss her?"

Josh pressed a tissue hard against his cut and stared down the sink drain. "Yes, we kissed a couple of times. Why are you asking me all this, Ben?"

"I just wonder sometimes, Josh."

"Wonder what?"

"I wonder if maybe you might have kissed Angie more than a couple of times if it wasn't for me."

Josh swiped a patch of fog from the mirror and grabbed another tissue for his eyes.

"I just wonder how you'll ever get married if you're always taking care of me," Ben fretted.

Ben didn't hear an answer from his brother, who had always answered before. He turned the shower head off and listened for a response.

"Josh?"

"Josh?" But there was not a sound above the last drip of water.

Ben wrapped himself in the towel and raced to find Josh. He found Josh standing outside the motel room door, leaning against the second-story railing and smoking a cigarette.

"Josh? I'm sorry. Sometimes I just say dumb things."

Josh took a long drag off the cigarette and motioned for Ben to join him leaning on the rail. "Look at that moon, Ben. That's the same moon that shined down on Momma and Daddy on the other side of that ocean we swam in today."

Ben's eyes widened to capture all the magnificence of that full moon.

"Somewhere in this world, Ben, there may be a girl looking at that moon right now that I would want to marry. But if I ever get married, I want it to be forever. And that's going to be tough if that girl isn't a lot like Momma."

Ben nodded in total understanding.

"I'm not sure Angie would have been that girl, Ben. Maybe we would have kissed more than a couple of times, but all I knew was that I wanted to be with you more than her."

Josh saw the tears forming in Ben's eyes and crushed out his cigarette under his shoe. "We're only twenty-three-years-old, Ben and forever is a long time. We're doing fine just thinking about today and dreaming about tomorrow. Now get your ass dressed and let's go eat."

The boys stormed the diner and ate their fill. Each bite was savored with extra dressing and extra sauce, and their waitress, Millie never let their glasses remain empty. Millie stopped by to offer dessert. She looked a bit like the boys' Grandma, with her silver hair tied up in a bun.

"Did you know a Jake and Cassie?" Ben blurted out. "They used to come here about 28 years ago."

Josh gave Ben a light kick in the shin, and Millie saw Josh's head wagging in shocked disapproval.

"Thanks for pointing out my age, Sonny," Millie playfully sneered.

Ben looked at Josh with eyes begging for help. "I'm sorry, Josh. I just said another dumb thing, didn't I?"

Millie tweaked Ben's ear and assured, "I'm just teasing, Honey. I've only been here a couple of years, but the bartender in the lounge has been here at least thirty years. Maybe you should ask him."

Ben was bursting with anticipation and Josh reached in his pocket for a handsome tip for a gracious lady. As the boys stood, Ben sincerely endeared, "I like your hair, Ma'am." Millie couldn't resist giving him the biggest hug he had gotten since he left Kansas.

The boys entered the lounge with a mixture of trepidation and anticipation. The lounge was darkly lit, and there was very little sound. The piano that once resided in the corner was gone. Mary Lou's fingers no longer graced the piano keys, and no one was singing. The boys sat at the bar and wondered what happened to the magic that Momma and Daddy had told them about.

The bartender approached, and his mouth flew open. "Oh, my God, Jake, you haven't aged a day!"

The boys looked at each other in bewilderment and then back at the bartender. He was a well-put-together man who had broadened with the passing of many years. He couldn't believe his eyes, and he couldn't close his mouth.

"I'm Josh, and this is my brother, Ben. But our Dad's name is Jake. He used to come in here a long time ago."

The bartender stared and inquired, "What, may I ask, is your Mom's name?"

"Cassie," Ben bubbled with uncontrollable love.

The bartender clutched his chest as if his heart was giving out. "Oh, Dear Lord!"

"Are you okay, Sir?" Josh was genuinely concerned.

The bartender reached out his hand, and Josh was the first to grab it. The bartender closed his eyes and remembered. "You've got your father's handshake."

Ben was beside himself. "Did you know our Mom and Dad, Sir?"

The bartender grasped Ben's hand and said, "Call me, Jeremy."

Ben shrank a bit and answered, "Our Daddy wouldn't like that, Sir."

"No, I suppose he wouldn't," Jeremy agreed. "What'll you boys have? Anything you want is on me."

"A couple of beers would be fine, Sir," Josh thanked.

"But Josh, the doctor said..." Ben resisted.

"One beer is not what's going to kill you, Ben," Josh settled.

Jeremy returned with the beers and leaned on the bar. "It was 1970. I know, because your parents are the reason I got back together with my wife."

The boys were spell-bound and clutched their beers tight. They had heard this story, but it was worth hearing again from someone who had been there and had seen.

"Mary Lou was playing the piano over there in the corner," Jeremy recollected, "and this young fella was singing his heart out. What was that song?"

"Ebb Tide, Sir," the boys answered in harmony.

"That's right! Ebb Tide," Jeremy clearly remembered. "Well, anyway, this young fella, your Dad, didn't have a great voice, but he was so into that song. He didn't notice the gorgeous young lady walk up behind him and join in singing the song."

"That was our Mom. Right Sir?" Ben panted.

"Yes, young man. And she had a voice. It seems she had just breezed into town to surprise your Dad. Now, your Dad thought she was five thousand miles away on the Island of – uh..."

"Guam, Sir," the boys gleefully filled in.

"That's right, Guam," Jeremy now recalled. "And your Dad thought he was just dreaming about her singing that song with him."

Jeremy had to pause while he laughed himself out of breath. He poured himself a glass of water and gulped and breathed. "Well, that last note took the roof off this place, and everyone in this room stood and cheered like – like everything was right with the world."

Jeremy had to pause again and breathe again. "Your Dad turned around and saw your Mom, and that embrace was what made me go back to my wife and find that same kind of love."

Josh was trying to swallow the lump in his throat, but Ben just let go and buried his face in Josh's shoulder.

Jeremy witnessed the love that had flowed from Jake and Cassie into these passionate boys and asked, "Say, what are your folks doing now?"

"Well," Josh began, "they drove long-haul trucks for a while, like Ben and me. Then they went back to Kansas and started "Eddie's Place.""

"Eddie's Place?" Jeremy was unfamiliar.

"Yes, Sir. It's a big farm where veterans can stay and work while they figure out what to do with the rest of their lives. There are thirty or forty vets there at a time, and they help each other get past the memories of war and find their way home."

Jeremy nodded his head and declared, "I knew those two were special."

The cocktail waitress came with an order, and Jeremy had to go. He walked away, shaking his fist and swearing, "I knew it."

The boys left the lounge that night with a whole new perspective on the moon that shined on them where ever they went.

Chapter 7

Sarah woke later than her normal a.m. routine. The alarm clock had sounded, but it could not shake the dreams that held Sarah hostage. They were dreams of what had been, what should have been, and what now should be. She could no longer think of Josh without seeing Ben. They were inseparable. It was that thought that made her eyes flutter open. "What happened to Ben?"

The alarm clock showed a startling 9:03 a. m. Sarah dove into her flip-flop slippers and gathered her papers. She didn't have time for a shower, and she had no patience for make-up. She snatched her car keys off the hook and ran as fast as her flip-flops would allow. She tested the limits of her car as she sped to Phillip McKay's office to drop off her report.

McKay's secretary, Amanda, saw the urgency in that young woman's stride as she bolted through the door. She could sense the crucial importance of the papers Sarah planted on her desk.

"Good morning, Sarah. Would you like to take those papers into Mr. McKay?"

"No," Sarah declined. "I have to meet Josh in an hour and a half, and I look like shit." Sarah didn't hear Amanda's parting guarantee as she propelled out the door. "I'll see that he gets this right away, Sarah. GO GIRL!"

Sarah used every bit of her time to make herself into what she wanted Josh to see. She showered and shampooed to show him what she wanted him to embrace. She applied make-up as if it was war-paint, to show that she was ready to fight for him.

She could hardly wait to hear the next chapter of Josh and Ben's story. She was amazingly awake, gulping the strongest coffee she could find to counteract a night of too much wine and too little sleep. Nothing was going to deter her from learning everything about two brothers whose love was greater than anything she had known.

Sarah arrived at the police station with a few minutes to spare. She expected to see Josh's face any moment, but the first face she saw was that of attorney Phillip McCay. He was seated at the table; over which Sarah had heard secrets that were meant for only her ears. McKay had Sarah's report, but he had questions and not enough answers. He stood and pulled out a chair. "Have a seat, Sarah."

Sarah sat in apprehensive, uncertain movements as if she was taking a seat in the principal's office. She intuitively covered her mouth with her fingers, locking in the secrets she held.

"Your report was very clinical and precise, Sarah, but it did not provide anything I can use to prepare a defense." McKay lowered his head to meet Sarah's downcast eyes. "You wouldn't be holding anything back, would you?"

Sarah tried to wag her head from left to right out of loyalty to Josh, but her head altered course and nodded in the affirmative. She needed McCay's allegiance and trust, and Josh needed all the help McCay could provide.

"He's from Kansas, and he lost a twin brother, named Ben." Sarah's head was now in her hands, and she was trembling at the thought of betraying Josh.

McCay laid a cautious hand on Sarah's shoulder. "Sarah?"

Sarah panted like a marathon runner and sat erect. "I am not supposed to get this emotionally attached, but…"

"Do you need to step away from this case, Sarah?" McCay suggested.

"NO!" Sarah rejected. "Josh needs me. And I need – I need to hear the rest of his story. I just need more time with him. Please!"

McCay pondered the legal implications of his next step. "Listen, Sarah. Attorney/client privilege extends only so far, but I can play dumb for a little while. We have less than a month before the court date. I need you to share everything you know, and I need you to learn everything you can as fast as you can."

This was a moment when truth was at odds with the desires that filled Sarah's heart. A choice had to be made between what was best for Josh and the confidence that she had promised. At risk was a bewildering bond she had found with a man whose love had no bounds. Sarah made her choice.

She reached into her satchel that held the beginning of Josh's story. She handed over the manuscript that had been crafted with the help of Cabernet Sauvignon. "His parents' names are Jake and Cassie, but he hasn't given me his last name. He will do anything to protect them from all of this. Please don't tell him I told you…"

The door opened, and Josh beamed at the sight of Sarah. Then his smile evaporated when he saw the stern, business-like look on McCay's face.

Detective Hallstrom followed Josh into the room, guided him into his chair, and initiated the conversation. "Counselor, do you have any information to share?"

McCay crossed his arms and responded in clear legal terms, "Miss Langston is developing a comprehensive profile of my client's personal background and recent activities. We have nothing pertinent to the charges you have filed, and my client retains his right to remain silent."

Hallstrom had expected a guarded response from a defense attorney, but he thought that Sarah might be a little more easily intimidated. He leaned across the table, a little too close to Sarah's face. Josh emitted a low growl and Hallstrom backed off to Josh's acceptable distance. "And you, Ms. Langston, surely Josh has been a bit more – uh – cooperative with you."

All eyes were on Sarah, but none could detect a flinch. "All of my findings have been provided to Josh's attorney." Sarah pulled her notepad out of her satchel and suggested, "I'm sure that Josh will share more in due time. And, this is our time, Detective."

Hallstrom turned his penetrating gaze on Josh. "You may have less time than you think, Josh."

Hallstrom confronted Josh again with the photo of the murder victim. Josh's fists involuntarily clinched, and the detective did not fail to notice. "He was driving a stolen car. We don't know his name yet either, but I'll bet you do."

Josh's head twitched and waggled. "The man in this picture is full of darkness."

"So, you knew this man!" Hallstrom attacked.

Josh closed his eyes and his body deflated. "I have known darkness."

"You don't have to answer any more questions today, Josh," McCay advised.

Hallstrom was astute enough to recognize a stand-off and sanctimoniously left the room. But, before closing the door, he poked his head back in and quipped, "Oh, Counselor, Ms. Langston, I'm sure you read in the police report that witnesses heard two gunshots. Perhaps you can ask Josh what he did with the gun."

A cloud filled the room after Hallstrom closed the door. For McCay, it was a cloud of mystery that had to be solved if he was ever going to defend a young man's life that hung in the balance. For Sarah, the cloud-shrouded the secrets she had to unlock if she was ever going to know what brought this young man into her life. For Josh, it was a cloud of his own making. It was a blanket, under which he was hiding. He couldn't allow anyone to unmask the degradation he had heaped on himself and his family's name.

McCay stood to give his account of where things stood. "Josh, I don't know if you understand how serious your situation is. We are still in this fight, but we need more from you, and we need it soon." McCay did not presume that his words would have any meaningful impact on Josh, but those words were all he had to offer before he left Sarah and Josh alone.

Sarah reached out, but Josh did not reach back. His elbows rocked on the table, as his fists thumped his head. "Josh? Talk to me, Josh."

Josh could not refuse Sarah's plea, but he had only one affection to share. "You can stop now, Sarah. It doesn't matter what happens now. They can't hurt me anymore."

"HURT YOU?" Sarah wailed. "WHAT ABOUT ME? YOU BIG DUMMY! Can't you tell how much I care about you?"

Josh jolted and bit his lip. "NO, Sarah. NO! You can't!"

Josh slammed his head hard against the table and tried to shake away the affection he could not court and the love that could never be.

"Don't you tell me what I can do and what I can't do, Josh," Sarah rebuked. "You tell me the rest of your story. ALL OF IT!"

Sarah opened her notebook and rested her chin on the table, next to Josh's ear. "What happened after Monterey?" she resolutely pushed.

Josh raised his head and rested his chin in front of Sarah's. He smoothed her hair back and could not resist that unyielding face. "Ben had more love than he could possibly hold in his heart. So, he gave it away to everyone he met. Most folks loved him back, but some couldn't see or feel who Ben was, and they tormented him."

Josh's tears were flowing faster and began to pool on the table around his chin. Sarah impassionedly daubed Josh's tears with her hair. "You can do it, Josh. Keep talking. Share that love with me."

Josh agonizingly sat upright with his eyes closed and sucked in all the courage he could muster. He reached for Sarah's delicate touch. He cradled her small hand between his powerful and calloused hands as if he was holding a baby bird. "I'll tell you who Ben was."

Sarah lightly rubbed those callouses, hoping to sooth the pain she was about to hear. Only brothers can experience the pain that flowed from Sarah's pen. Only brothers can know the bond that Josh and Ben shared. The next chapter that Sarah would write would require something a little stronger than wine.

Chapter 8

Session 2
11:20 am, September 19, 2001

The boys left Monterey on schedule, allowing enough time to bathe in the Pacific Ocean once more on their way to Los Angeles. They saw all the sights and wonders that Momma and Daddy had described, and a few more.

Josh was on a mission. He and Ben were going to see all fifty states. Most people never see all fifty states, regardless of how long they live. If Ben was not going to live as many years as most folks do, Josh was determined that Ben's short years would be full of life.

Los Angeles was big and bright and exciting, but it wasn't home. It was just a stop in their whirlwind adventure.

Disneyland was more their style, and the boys spent two days being nine years old again. Ben's face lit up like Christmas morning at all the sights and sounds of fantasy land. On each ride, Josh's eyes were fixed on Ben's jubilant smile. And nothing from cotton candy to snow cones was outside their budget.

When the boys hit the road again, they were filled to the brim with corn dogs and curly fries and life was better than good. It was the life they had dreamed about, and it was the life they were making happen.

The boys didn't always get along, and times were not always joyful. Ben didn't like Josh's smoking, and Josh didn't like Ben's farting. Ben knew the route dictated by the map, and Josh knew the route he wanted to take.

There were blown-out tires and clogged fuel lines. There was bad weather that could not be defeated, and there was fatigue and sleepiness that could not be ignored. The boys fought with each other, and they fought together, and no one should dare to ever come between them.

They rode all night to reach Phoenix on time to drop off their load. All they wanted was a big breakfast and a bed. They found Momma and Daddy's favorite truck stop and diner and ordered the breakfast they had earned.

The boys were not identical twins, but their breakfast orders were always exactly the same. Two scrambled eggs with another egg fried over-easy was a given. The hash browns had to be extra crispy and topped with salsa. The meat was not a choice, it was a requirement. Ham, sausage, and bacon, they wanted them all. If the orange juice was not freshly squeezed, then tomato juice was preferred. Keep the coffee coming and expect a handsome tip.

"I've got to hit the can, Ben. I'll be right back."

"Ok, Josh. But don't be surprised if I steal your eggs."

Josh chuckled on his way to the men's room. "Three eggs plus two eggs equals five eggs."

He had taught Ben that first math lesson, gathering eggs from the chicken house. He had taught Ben everything he could and loved him all he could. If Ben wanted his eggs, they were his to have.

Josh finished his business in the men's room but took a little extra time to splash water in his face. Josh was weary. Wearier than a young man should be. He had fought so many battles in defense of his brother. He had declined so many pleasures that were within his grasp for the greater good of his brother. But that was all he knew how to do.

He splashed another double-handful of water and searched his own eyes in the mirror. "Am I strong enough? Am I brave enough?" All Josh knew was that he loved enough.

As the bathroom door closed behind Josh, he saw two big, burly truck drivers standing next to Ben. Josh could see the taunting look in their eyes. He had seen it far too many times, beginning with the Miller boys who tried to bully Ben in the first grade.

Josh knew their type all too well. Sure, they were big and strong, but they were cowards looking for easy prey.

One of the cowards took a long, deep drag off his cigarette and blew the smoke in Ben's face. He flicked the ash over Ben's eggs and then dropped the cigarette butt into Ben's coffee cup.

Ben was helplessly petrified. He didn't know whether to run or fight or just cry. He looked around frantically for Josh and quaked.

Josh was on the run, as the two cowards headed to the cash register to settle their bill. Josh's first instinct was to stop and grab Ben's quivering face. "Go get in the truck, Ben."

Josh held Ben's face and waited for a response. But Ben knew what was going to happen. Josh was getting ready to fight another battle for him, and Josh was telling him to run.

"NO, JOSH! NO MORE! I'm not going to run. I don't want the bastards to win."

Josh saw the fury in Ben's eyes, which he had rarely seen before. Ben's breathing slowed and grew deeper with conviction. "I don't want to be afraid anymore, Josh. But I don't know how to fight. Show me, Josh."

Josh was humbled by the courage he heard in his brother's voice. It was the courage of a little guy who didn't care about the odds of victory or defeat. The right or wrong of what might come next was blurred. But the hurt that had been dished out to Ben was just WRONG.

"Follow me, Ben," Josh gave way.

The boys met the two cowards head-on and blocked their way to the door. Josh spread his feet into a firm, steady stance. Ben cranked his head around to loosen the muscles in his neck.

The big, burly cowards were amused. They laughed at the sight of one sturdy man and one stunted freak.

Josh began with a diversion. "Ben, you take the guy on the left."

The guy on the left diverted his eyes to the stunted freak, and Josh landed a left jab on his nose. The guy on the left reeled and stumbled, and Josh landed a right jab to the guy on the right. In just two more punches, the guy on the right was the guy on the floor.

Josh looked back to the guy on the left, as Ben pounded him with relentless punishment. Ben was not strong, and Ben was not fast. But Ben was on fire.

Ben was pounding the Miller boys who bullied him in the first grade. He was kicking at all the sneers and laughs that had tormented him throughout his life. He unleashed everything bottled up inside him until the guy on the left was another guy on the floor.

Ben dropped to his knees, swayed with a dazed look in his eyes, and took one more deep breath. He muttered all that breath would allow, "I'm sorry, Gretchen."

Josh caught Ben before his head hit the floor and screamed, "CALL AN AMBULANCE!"

Josh cradled Ben's head and talked to him as he always did. "Ben, listen to me, Ben. Are you listening, Ben? You won, Ben. The bastards didn't win. You did."

Ben couldn't talk. He could barely breathe. But Josh could see life still fighting behind those eyelids. "DON'T YOU DARE LEAVE ME, BEN!"

The minutes were excruciating until the paramedics arrived. It was incredibly hard for Josh to let go, to stand back, and to place his brother's life in someone else's hands.

The paramedics employed their skills to stabilize Ben's palpitating heart and pumped oxygen into his lungs. "Is he on any special medication for his heart?" the paramedic asked.

"Yes, Sir," Josh stammered. "He takes – uh - I don't know the names, but we have a bag full of pills in the truck."

"Go get them, son," the paramedic directed.

That was the best thing that Josh could have heard. It was exactly what he needed, something he could do for his brother. He streaked across the parking lot, and his tears streamed backward as he pushed against the wind.

Josh had lost a couple of races in his time, but no one could have beaten him that day. No promise of the fame and glory of victory would have been a match for Josh's drive. He was running to save the better half of himself. He was running to save what defined himself. He was running as if his own life depended on it because it did.

Josh retrieved the bag full of pills and Ben's folder of medical records and headed back, without pausing for one wasted breath. A police patrol car had pulled up in front of the diner and blocked his way. Josh sailed over the hood of the car and blasted his way through the front door.

He dumped the bag of pills at the feet of the paramedic and started to grab them one-by-one. "This bottle with the red cap is for his heart. And this – this blue cap is for his lungs. This brown cap – this is for his digestive system. He's my brother. You've gotta..."

"Calm down, son," the paramedic stilled. "We have the doctor on the phone. Your brother is going to be fine."

Two police officers entered the diner with their hands on their pistol butts. One officer intercepted the two cowards as they attempted to limp out the door. The other officer stood behind the young man who had sailed over the hood of his patrol car and tapped him on the shoulder.

Josh spun and went into his fighting stance again. His fists clenched, and every muscle tensed in preparation for the next round to be fought. But he saw a pair of eyes that made his fists unclench.

It wasn't the sergeant stripes on the sleeve that made Josh relax his muscles. It wasn't the badge on the chest that made him feel safe. It was the eyes of Gabriel Sandoval that made him melt into the strong arms of a trusted friend.

Gabriel Sandoval was one of the hundreds of vets that Josh and Ben had grown up with. He had spent many months at "Eddie's Place." He had fought the haunting demons of war, and the demons had lost. He had worked the fields of the Kansas farm and watched two young boys run free through a life worth living.

"JOSH!" Gabriel exclaimed.

"GABE! Help me, Gabe!" Josh pleaded. "Ben's in trouble!"

Gabriel squeezed young Josh in his arms and looked at Ben. He saw the needles and tubes delivering life back into the body of the boy that had taught him so much about courage. He could almost feel the heartbeat of the boy that had taught him so much about devotion.

Gabriel called to his partner. "Call for back-up. Get all the witness statements you can. I'm going to be sticking with these two boys."

Ben was wheeled to the ambulance, and Gabriel, and Josh could not be held back from riding along. Ben was in and out between sleep and consciousness. But whether his eyelids were open or closed, his eyes were searching for Josh.

"Josh!" Ben cried out.

"I'm here, Ben. You're going to be ok."

"Josh!"

"Yeah, Ben?"

"Tell Gretchen I'm sorry, Josh."

"You're going to tell her, Ben. You hang in there, and you tell her."

Ben drifted back into his restless sleep, and Josh stroked the hair of the boy who had been by his side since they left their mother's womb.

"Is that your sister, Gretchen he's talking about?" Gabriel assumed.

"Yeah, Gabe," Josh confirmed. "Gretchen is a Navy chaplain now. She's somewhere in the Persian Gulf. She taught Ben all the stories about Jesus and all the songs. She taught him to turn the other cheek and love your enemy."

Josh rested his brow on Ben's chest and cried, "He wants Gretchen to forgive him, but I'm the one that needs forgiveness, Gabe. I took my brother into that fight, and I threw the first punch."

Gabriel stroked Josh's back in concert with his heaving sobs. Gabriel had thrown many a punch in defense of a brother, and he remembered having taught Josh that there was no such thing as a fair fight. When you're fighting for your brother, make sure you throw the first punch.

"But you should have seen him, Gabe," Josh bragged. "He was something else. Ben didn't want to run anymore, and he didn't want to be laughed at anymore."

Josh laced his fingers into Ben's hair. "And they weren't laughing anymore, Gabe. He put that bastard down."

It was a couple more miles to the hospital, and Gabriel offered, "I'll contact your folks for you, Josh."

Ben's eyes flew open, and he pleaded, "NO! Please no. I don't want Momma and Daddy to come - come and take me home. Josh and I have nineteen - nineteen more states to see."

Ben clutched Josh's shirt. "Please, Josh. I want to tell them about Albuquerque - and Amarillo and about – uh…"

"Oklahoma City, Ben."

"Yeah – and – Joplin and Wichita."

Josh knew that he couldn't promise anything anymore. All he could do was look Ben straight in the eyes and nod and hold his hand to his chest.

Ben's heart was still racing when the emergency room took him under their care. IVs were inserted, and monitors were attached. But all that modern medicine could offer was no match for Josh's grip on his brother's hand.

Josh ignored the demands that he leave the room. No surgery could have separated the boys who had been joined since birth.

"Ben? Are you listening to me, Ben?"

The monitor registered a spike in Ben's respiration.

"We need to get back on the road again, Ben. We're running a little late."

Ben's respiration slowed, and his heart slowed.

"I need you to show me the way to Albuquerque, Ben."

Ben couldn't raise his arm or direct his hand, but his finger pointed to the window, that just happened to face east.

Josh never left his brother's side, except when nature called. Then he was back to the only place he ever belonged. To feel Ben's pulse was all that mattered. No one and nothing could ever replace that.

Three more hours of faithful vigilance were all that Josh could handle. He lay his head on Ben's rib cage, but never let go of his hand. "I'm going to take a nap now, Ben. Wake me when it's time to go."

Josh drifted through endless dreams of childhood and manhood. Every dream included Ben. There could be no dreams without him.

The monitors recorded the strength within Ben. His heartbeat became steady and refused to give up. His breathing found purpose, and his eyes fluttered open.

"Josh?"

Josh bolted to his feet and looked at his brother's face. "Yeah, Ben?"

"I put the fuel cap back on, Josh. Don't worry."

Josh placed his hand on Ben's brow. He mouthed a quiet prayer to the Lord, who had given him back his life. Then, he responded, "You did good, Ben. We're ready to go."

Ben was kept in the hospital for two more days of observation. Tests were run, and doctors consulted. The boys listened to the same dismal prognosis they had heard before. They listened to the same recommendations for bedrest, special diet, and more needles and tests.

But on the third day, Josh wheeled his brother out of the hospital and helped boost him into the truck. They were not going to waste one more minute in the hospital that spoke of impending death. They were going to capture every minute of life.

Sergeant Gabriel Sandoval shouted to the boys as they pulled away. "ASK YOUR FOLKS IF I COULD SHOW UP FOR THANKSGIVING."

Ben leaned half of his body out the window. "JUST BE THERE, GABE."

Sarah's pen trailed off the page, leaving a scribble after that last sentence she wrote. The Jack Daniel's had dulled her senses, but her heart would not let her release her grip on the pen. She had spent all of herself for tonight, and only the healing power of sleep and her irresistible dreams would see her through until morning.

Chapter 9

Sarah's dreams were interrupted by the same enticing rays of sun that roused Josh from his implausible fantasies. His whimsies of what could never be gave way to the reality that today might be all he would ever have. But today he would see Sarah again, and today would be his best day.

Isn't that where we all need to be? Tomorrow is only a dream. Today is all that we have. It's our one shot at making yesterday's dreams come true. Sarah might not be in Josh's future, but she would be his today.

Sarah's first thoughts were somewhat longer in range. For her, today was her best shot at making tomorrow happen. She was determined to learn more about Josh's yesterdays, and for their future, forever was the only acceptable option.

Sarah and Josh's affections were all they had to share. The unforgiving world that threatened to tear them apart was nipping at their heels. The relentless wheels of justice were grinding, and nothing would stop them.

While Sarah brushed her teeth in anticipation of her next enchanted encounter with a love she knew only as Josh, plans were being laid to rip him out of her life. As Josh combed his hair, officers of the law were plotting to put him away. As Sarah and Josh looked in the mirror in search of each other's face, Detective Hallstrom opened the file of evidence that might end the greatest love story that might have been.

Hallstrom was making painfully slow progress, trying to identify the murder victim. He had been driving a stolen car, which had been traced to its owner in Macon, Georgia. The ID found on the victim was likely also stolen, and he had no lead as to the contents of that rolled up blanket flung across Josh's shoulder as he fled the murder scene. Hallstrom had given up trying to get information from Josh but was not about to give up on the investigation of Josh's obvious guilt.

Attorney McCay knocked on Hallstrom's open door and invited himself in. "No, Detective, I have no information to share with you today."

"I'm not surprised, Counselor," Hallstrom dismissed.

"Well," McCay regretted. "That is a matter of concern for me as well. I need information to put together a defense, and it's just not there."

"I would imagine it's a greater concern for you, Counselor," Hallstrom patronized.

"I have the fibers matching Josh's jacket, and I can advance the strong theory that he was the last person to see the victim alive. I don't think you have anything, and I doubt that young man will ever divulge even his plea of guilty or innocent."

"That's why I'm here, Detective. I need to speak with Sarah before you bring Josh in. I need to impress upon her how imperative it is that she push a little harder."

Hallstrom pointed down the hall. "Here she comes now, Counselor. Good luck."

McCay stepped into the hall and greeted, "Good Morning, Sarah. I see you're right on time."

"I wouldn't miss it for the world," Sarah declared.

McCay escorted Sarah into the room and had her take a seat at the table she had been sharing with Josh for days of increasing connection. Then, he paced with his arms crossed and one hand touching his chin. "Eddie's Place is a home for struggling veterans."

"That's right," Sarah concurred. "That was in my report to you."

"It's on a farm near Hays, Kansas," McCay enlightened.

Sarah became positively giddy. She had wanted to track that information down, but she had been busy day and night, listening to Josh and writing his story.

McCay leaned on the table, so he could watch Sarah's eyes. "Eddie's Place is operated by a Jake and Cassie Marshall."

Sarah did not disappoint McCay. He watched the fireworks exploding in Sarah's eyes. "Josh Marshall," Sarah swooned. "Josh Marshall!"

Sarah leapt into a twirl and danced her way into McCay's arms. "Thank you, thank you, thank you."

McCay guided Sarah back to her chair and stilled her with his hands on her shoulders. His forbidding glare forewarned that it was not yet time to celebrate. "Now comes the tough part."

McCay stepped to the door and stuck his head out. "Officer, please have the prisoner, Josh brought in now."

"Oh, Lord!" Sarah realized. "If we tell Josh that we know his last name, he's going to think I betrayed him."

"That's why I'm going to talk to him first, Sarah. I'm going to be tough on him, and I need you to be strong for him."

"But we can't - I can't," Sarah wailed.

McCay held Sarah's face in his gentle grasp, as you would not expect from your attorney. The tender kiss on her forehead was more than a colleague's assurance. It was a wholehearted promise. "Trust me, Sarah. Stand with me and stand with Josh."

Sarah could not help the lurch that overtook her when she saw Josh standing in the doorway. His usual ear-to-ear grin greeted the grimace on her face. Her frown was not what he had hoped to see, but it was still the face he loved.

Josh noted the stern composure in McCay's posture and offered a cordial, yet cautious, "Hello. I'm not sure if I should be glad to see you."

"Have a seat, Josh," McCay coaxed.

Josh sat with his hands in the middle of the table as always, and Sarah naturally grabbed them tight.

"What's wrong, Sarah?" Josh detected. "Your eyes always change a little in color when something's wrong."

"What's wrong," McCay intervened, "is that we are running out of time Mr. Marshall."

Josh slid backward, and his chair screeched and slammed against the wall. He yanked his hands out of Sarah's. "Oh, Josh, PLEASE!" Sarah weakly begged.

Josh's eyes darted around the room, from Sarah to McCay, to the door, and to the officer on the other side of the glass who had his hand on the doorknob.

"You have not been betrayed, Josh," McCay quickly asserted. "No one else knows your last name. But as easy as it was for me to find out, I'm sure the police will discover your identity soon. Your family will eventually find out."

"NOooo!" Josh screamed as he bounded from his chair and hid his face in the corner. He pounded the walls until his knuckles bled.

The officer opened the door and stepped in. "It's alright, Officer," McCay protected.

The officer observed the violent, yet only self-destructive behavior of a man in excruciating torment. "Josh?" his familiar voice echoed.

It was the voice that had granted Josh a shave and a haircut. It was a voice to be trusted, and it was a voice that deserved a response.

But Josh could not respond. He couldn't even stand. His knees gave way, and he slumped into the lowest depth of that corner. He was as low in stature as a man can be, but he was not alone.

Sarah's tiny body enveloped that cringing ball of sobs. Neither light nor sound could pierce the passion she wrapped around her heart's desire. Only the touch of Sarah's hands could soothe the pain that Josh could hardly bear. Only the coo in Sarah's voice could lessen the despair that gripped Josh's soul.

Officer Crenshaw was a witness of the humanity of this sobering moment. He felt the gravity that pressed down on two kindred souls that wanted nothing but to love. He withdrew from the room and resumed his place on the other side of the glass.

"Josh," McCay reasoned, "I'm sure your family would rather see you in the flesh now, rather than behind prison bars or possibly six feet under. Don't let this be all about you, Josh. Let it be about your family. They need to hear from you. They need to see you and touch you. They need to know that you're going to be ok."

Josh's muffled voice resonated in the corner. "I told you I don't need a lawyer. You're fired. Now, leave me alone."

McKay pulled out a chair and sat with his arms crossed in unimpeachable authority. "There's a problem with you firing me, Josh," McCay advised. "I am retained by Ms. Sarah Langston, my only niece."

Josh spun and planted his back into the corner. He searched Sarah's eyes for confirmation. "Sarah?"

"Yes, Josh, he's my Uncle Phil," Sarah endeared. "And Josh, I was hoping you would introduce me to your family."

Josh's eyes softened into a hint of a smile, as his heart and mind captured a moment of clarity. A future worth fighting for was kneeling in front of him, and she wanted to meet his family. "You would just love them, Sarah."

"I know I will, Josh."

McCay looked over his shoulder to ensure the officer had left the room and that the door was still closed. "I can help you, Josh, but you need to help me. I need you to tell me one thing now. And, no matter what your answer is, I will believe you, and I will defend you."

Uncle Phil stood and crossed the room. He knelt behind Sarah and asked in unretractable confidence, "Did you kill that man?"

Josh pushed himself harder into the corner, and his face shattered. Sarah embraced that contorted face. "I'm never going away, Josh. We can fight this together."

Josh buried his face in the crook of Sarah's neck. McCay could see, and Sarah could feel the slow, painful nod of, "Yes."

"Well," McCay counseled, "now we know what we're dealing with. You just took your first step home, Josh."

McCay had no further words to offer. Words were not what Josh needed. Only Sarah's touch could bandage the wounds to Josh's heart. McCay rose and quietly left the room, armed with the knowledge he needed to prepare for battle.

Hallstrom did not miss the chance to stand in McCay's way. "Well, Counselor, any luck?"

"Yes, Detective, I have just discovered that I am defending a man who is innocent of murder."

McCay sidestepped around his professional adversary and strolled down the hall. Hallstrom spun and shouted after him, "Are you talking an insanity plea – self-defense – what?"

"Good-day, Detective."

Sarah persuasively guided Josh out of the corner, and with the toughness of love, commanded him to resume their familiar pose across the table. That's what makes love work. When your soulmate is hurting and clinging to his last 10 percent of strength, you have to make up the difference with 200 percent of devotion.

Sarah reached into her satchel and brought out a tape recorder. Josh flinched at the sight, but Sarah assured, "This will help us move through your story a little faster. But you're not talking to the machine, Josh, you're talking to me."

Josh needed a few more minutes to come back to the present. The past was in that corner that shriveled his hope. The future that he could not imagine sat right in front of him.

"But, I still don't know if I can talk about – about that day, Sarah."

"We were talking about Ben," Sarah steered. "Weren't you boys just leaving Phoenix?"

Sarah massaged Josh's temples until memories started pouring out of him. She giggled at the fondest memories and sighed at the hard ones. She shared the joys with a smile and bolstered up her will to listen to the sorrows. And, she never let go of Josh. The tape recorder did all the work, while Sarah gave all the love.

She didn't push, and she didn't prod. She just listened. Every word that Josh wrenched out of his gut was recorded in magnetic bits and burned into Sarah's heart.

Chapter 10

That evening, in Sarah's lonely apartment, she poured herself a glass of wine, but never took a sip. She poured a glass for Josh and set it next to hers. That helped her feel that Josh was there with her, as she listened to the tape recording and transcribed the voice that would not leave her head.

Wine can be such a sweet melancholy for a soul that is searching for a place to rest. The sparkle of the light through the glass can illuminate the darkest of places, while the deep red color of the wine can subdue the darkest of thoughts. Sarah melded into that subdued sparkle as she listened again to the continued story of Josh and Ben.

Session 3
9:00 am, September 20, 2001

The boys missed their load out of Phoenix, but they found the next load in Albuquerque. Ben didn't do any more lifting or loading. Josh would not allow it. But Ben kept moving. No power on earth was going to keep him from checking the oil and the air pressure in the tires. He would not surrender his job of keeping the windshield and mirrors clean. He just had to keep moving.

Ben got his prescribed bed rest, to the soothing rumble of eighteen wheels carrying him through worlds he had only dreamed of. He was quieter these days. He didn't want to miss seeing anything, from red bluffs to the painted desert, from cities and towns to the people, and the places they called home.

Josh was different too. He had learned more courage from his brother than he had ever found on his own. He had learned that he could no longer fight all his brother's battles for him. But he had found more questions than answers.

What could he do to ease his brother's struggle? What could he do for a young man who had never hurt anyone before, and now felt shame for having stood up for himself?

"You know, Ben," Josh broached the topic, "we don't have to tell Gretchen about that fight back in Phoenix. You didn't do anything wrong, and I was really proud of you."

A tumbleweed rolled across the Texas prairie and bounced off the hood of the truck. "Wow! Did you see that, Josh?" Ben avoided.

"Ben?" Josh persisted.

Ben kept his eyes on the tumbleweed, rolling along its unintended and carefree path. "Yeah, I do, Josh. I have to tell her."

Ben twisted around in his seat and spoke his heart directly to Josh. "I've had more friends than enemies, Josh. But I forgot that back there in Phoenix. I forgot what Gretchen taught me."

"What did she teach you, Ben? Teach me."

Ben pressed his hands over his eyes and tried to remember every word. "She said - there is more good than evil in this world. She said the good is the light – and – the evil is the darkness."

Ben began to rock and press his hands tighter against his eyes.

"Take your time, Ben. Remember the words."

"She said – the darkness cannot – cannot defeat the light. She said – don't try to fight darkness with – with darkness. Stay on the side of the light."

Ben had only memorized those words before, but now he knew what they meant. Josh also understood a little more, and a couple more questions were answered.

"Maybe we both need to tell Gretchen what we learned," Josh acknowledged.

The next couple hundred miles were the quietest the boys had ever been. They knew where they had come from, and they knew where they were going. They had come from the same womb, and they were traveling the same road. They had fought their way this far together. As the miles disappeared under the truck, miles stretched before them, and happy or sad, those miles belonged to them.

Their next stop was in Amarillo, and that is where their boundless joy was reborn. Ben had finished all his truck stop duties. The windshield was gleaming, and he had thumped every tire. He was standing behind Josh as Josh tightened the cap on the fuel tank.

"Don't forget, Josh."

"Do I ever forget, Ben?"

Josh headed in to pay for the fuel and looked back to see Ben grabbing a fist-full of paper towels and the windshield scrubber. Ben scurried around the truck and began cleaning a spot on the back door of the trailer. It was the spot just to the right of the sticker that said, "New Mexico – Land of Enchantment."

Ben was dancing as if he had to go pee when Josh returned with the sticker that said, "Don't Mess with Texas." Josh steadied Ben as he climbed to paste the thirty-third sticker.

"How many more states to go, Josh?"

"Climb down, Ben, and we'll figure it out together."

The boys sat on the curb next to the fuel pumps and opened their cold cans of cola. "How many more states did you say we had left to go when we were in Phoenix?" Josh asked before he took a big swig. He always gave Ben plenty of time to remember, and Ben would get there in his own precious time.

"Nineteen?" Ben responded with a little less than certainty.

"That's right, Ben, nineteen. And when we stopped in Albuquerque, we added one more sticker."

"The Land of Enchantment!" Ben spewed.

Josh chuckled and choked a little on the next gulp and nodded his head. "And you just added, "Don't Mess with Texas." Now all you need to do is subtract two from nineteen. Just count backward, Ben."

Ben concealed his hands between his knees, so Josh wouldn't see him using his fingers. "Nineteen-eighteen–seven...- seventeen states to go! Let's get going, Josh."

Ben didn't need a boost to mount his seat in the truck. He was waiting for Josh to get behind the wheel and pointed east when he heard the engine roar. Ben began turning the dial on the radio, pausing to hear if the music matched the good day that had just started. He always loved finding a song that Josh just couldn't resist singing along with, and he hit the jackpot. The radio was playing Marty Robbins' songs.

Josh did not hold back. He knew every word, and every note was pure gold to Ben's ears.

The boys diverted their route, turning south, toward Fort Worth, where Grandma and Grandpa had raised their mother, Cassie. It added 281 miles to their travels, but they had been taught that if you are ever within a couple hundred miles of your family, stop in to pay them a visit.

They spent only one night with Grandma and Grandpa, but it was a night full of memories and love. The past was remembered, and the present was celebrated. Ben was so excited. "We're going to Oklahoma City next, Grandma. They call that the "Sooner State." Then we're going to Joplin. Missouri is called the "Show Me State." Did you know that, Grandpa?"

The Grandparents nodded, not so much in acknowledgment of Ben's breadth of knowledge, but more so in adulation of Ben's zest for life.

It was as hard as ever when the boys said farewell to two old folks who had said their share of farewells.

The boys left as soon as the sun made its daily debut. It was a great day, and it was a great song on the radio. They were about three hours away from their next drop-off in Oklahoma City when the sweet sounds of music on the radio abruptly stopped.

"We interrupt this broadcast with an important message. The Texas State Department of Public Safety has issued an Amber Alert for the Greater Dallas area. A twelve-year-old Melinda Miles may be traveling in a dark blue Ford Ranger, Texas License Plate BC5-X489. If you have any information, please call 911."

Ben was shaking and could barely control the pen he put to paper. "BC5 - what were the rest of the numbers, Josh?"

"I didn't catch them, Ben. Just calm down, Buddy."

"But, Josh, it's an Amber Alert! It was a blue Ford, right?" Ben's eyes were darting from his pad of paper to Josh and then to the road.

"You have to calm down, Ben. We'll keep our eyes open, but don't get your hopes up. There's only a slight chance that we can help."

"NO!" Ben refused to believe. "We have to find her!"

Josh could see the tell-tale signs of Ben's palpitating heart and his hyperventilating breaths. Josh couldn't wait for the next exit. He turned the flashers on and pulled to the side of the Interstate.

He rummaged through the bag of pills and found the bottle with the red cap. "We're going to take one of these, Ben. Hold your breath now. Come on, Ben, look at me."

Ben's focus was blurring, but he turned toward the voice that had been by his side all his life.

Josh placed a hand behind Ben's head and drew their foreheads together. "Hold your breath."

Ben quivered a breath and held it while Josh counted, "One-two-three. Now let it out, Brother. That's it, let it all out. Now let's hold the next breath till the count of five."

This was one of countless times the boys had breathed together and shared sips of water until Ben could swallow his pill.

Josh backed his head away, so Ben could focus on his eyes, but he kept a firm grip on the back of Ben's neck. "Remember when the cow got out of the pasture, and we couldn't find her?"

Ben nodded at the memory he had always held.

"Then what did we do, Ben?"

Ben's eyes lit up as the memory flooded his mind. "We called all the family to help. And – and all the vets - came to help."

"There must have been forty people out looking for that cow, huh, Ben?"

"Yeah," Ben jubilantly recalled. "And we-we found the cow, Josh."

"Yes, we did, Ben. But that was forty people looking around a couple of square miles."

Josh leaned back in his seat and pointed down the highway. "That road seems to go forever, and there are lots more roads. There are hundreds of thousands of square miles out here to search. We can't do it alone."

Ben's brow wrinkled as he looked around as far as the eye could see. His posture shriveled into a dejected slump.

"But that's what the Amber Alert is for, Ben. There will be hundreds of people looking out for a dark blue Ford Ranger."

Ben grabbed his pen and paper and added "Dark blue Ford Ranger."

"I have to tell you, though, Ben, sometimes they find missing kids, but sometimes they don't."

Ben's face puckered, and a tear fell onto his pad of paper.

"We'll just keep our eyes peeled, Ben," Josh guaranteed. "Now, if Gretchen was here with us, what would she do?"

Ben closed his eyes and rocked and prayed. That's what Gretchen would do. As long as Ben rocked and prayed, he was out of danger, and Josh threw in the clutch.

The boys stopped at the first opportunity and called to find out the full license plate number of that dark blue Ford Ranger. That was the first of many numbers Ben clipped to the visor. There would be other missing children in newspapers and posters, and Ben would keep notes on each one. Ben would be ever watchful, hoping that one day he would find a little girl or boy that needed to go home.

Ben pasted another sticker on the back of the truck in Oklahoma City, and another in Joplin. They didn't pause or hesitate after fueling in Wichita. They were only three hours from home. Three hours of hauling ass would get them back to the arms of the family they had left three months ago.

The boys made it home well before Thanksgiving, and the party began. It began around the fire pit at "Eddie's Place." Dozens of vets, family, and friends shared the food that had always brought them together. They danced around the blazing fire that had always fueled their spirts, and then everyone gathered around to listen to Ben's stories.

Grandma Marshall was listening with her eyes closed. Behind those eyelids, she saw memories of days gone by. She saw two boys who had given her the joy of today and the promise of tomorrow. Her ears perceived the love she had given that was now being repaid through Ben's words.

Jake and Cassie heard their own lives being retold in stories of the open road. And they remembered every blessing of having raised two boys, neither of which would ever leave his brother behind.

The dozens of vets relished their recollections of better days. Their spirits were uplifted by Ben's testimony that the best days were yet to come.

Ben regaled them all with accounts of adventures in Denver and Salt Lake City. He described perfectly the sights and wonders in Seattle and Portland. He even told them all about the guy who forgot to replace the fuel cap in Salem. The only story Ben did not tell was about two cowardly bastards in Phoenix. That story would have to wait for only Gretchen's ears.

Gretchen arrived only one day before Thanksgiving, and her time home would be brief. She could never stay long when she had sailors and airmen who needed Chaplain Gretchen Marshall's spiritual strength.

Gretchen, Ben, and Josh sat on the bank of the farm pond as they had so many times and not so long ago. Memories of childhoods shared did not need to be spoken. The breeze across the pond carried them all.

But Gretchen could see the anguish in Ben's face, and she remembered well how Josh looked across the water in silence whenever trouble had crossed their path. She prompted Ben with, "Fear not, little flock. It is the Father's good pleasure..."

Ben gave an instant and innocent response "to give you the Kingdom."

"Tell me, Little Brother, what's in your heart?"

Ben cried through his complete account of the bullies in Phoenix. With a mix of shame and pride, he told about his failure to turn the other cheek and about how he put the bastard on the floor. He was so proud, yet so confused. All he could say was, "I'm sorry, Gretchen."

Gretchen cradled Ben's head on her shoulder and softly asked, "Do you have anything to add, Josh?"

Josh shuffled his feet and continued to gaze across the water. "Nah, it was just like Ben said."

Gretchen hummed to Ben for a moment, and Ben could feel the soothing vibrations from her neck. "I don't have all the answers, boys. All I can tell you is what I know."

Ben looked up at Gretchen's face and tuned his ear to her every word. "Joshua fought the battle of Jericho, and God was on his side. God strengthened Sampson, and with the jaw bone of an ass, Sampson slew the Philistines."

Josh was nodding in agreement and self-justification. But Ben was still confused.

Gretchen continued with how Jesus taught us a new way of life and a new path to salvation. "Jesus showed us how to "offer the other cheek as well," all the way to the cross. And he said, "Blessed are you when people insult you, persecute you and falsely say all kinds of evil against you because of me."

Ben was riveted in Gretchen's arms, and Josh was fighting back a tear.

Gretchen disclosed, "I am asked all the time by military troops, "Why should I fight? Why should I die? What am I fighting for?"

Gretchen paused and sternly ordered, "Josh, get over here." Josh complied and knelt on one knee in front of his brother and sister.

Gretchen wrapped her hands around a hand from Josh and a hand from Ben. "Remember what you learned at a very young age. The only good reason for fighting with your brother is so you can learn how to fight for him."

Gretchen could feel the grip tighten in both boys' hands. "And Jesus gave us His answer. "There is no greater love than this than to lay down one's life for a friend."

That was something both boys could understand. That was at the core of their belief. That was the motto they had lived by through thick and thin. That was the creed that had sustained them through childhood, adolescence, and tens of thousands of miles.

Gretchen had always been able to share her faith in ways that helped the boys live in grace and in peace. Now she gave them the most important challenge.

"So, boys, the only question you will ever need to ask yourself is, what am I fighting for."

That made sense to Josh, and he could live with that advice. Ben would ponder the meaning for some time, but he would live by his sister's words. Gretchen blessed Ben with a kiss on the ear and Josh with a kiss on the nose. She concluded, "Let's go see if there's any pie left."

After the last pumpkin pie had been devoured, the boys hit the road again. They had been taught to never say good-bye. They said farewell to family and friends that would always be in their thoughts, and they hugged the daylights out of their sister who would be ever-present in their hearts.

This was the easiest chapter for Sarah to write. Ben was still alive. Hope was alive. Courage and compassion prevailed. Sarah knew that darker times were coming, but for now, she could sleep. She could dream without sorrow or fear. And she could love like she had never loved before.

Chapter 11

At Josh and Sarah's next rendezvous, Sarah thought she knew Ben, but she had only scratched the surface. She thought she knew Gretchen, but there was so much more to know. Her greatest desire was to know everything about this young man, Josh who spoke of nothing but love.

But Josh had said all he wanted to say about Ben. What he wanted was to ask, "What's your favorite color, Sarah?"

Sarah laid her pen down, closed her eyes and cherished, "All the earth tones, brown, green, yellow, and in the Fall, red. What about you, Josh? What's your favorite color?"

"Whatever color your eyes are. What is that color?"

Sarah resisted her inclination to wrap her arms around Josh's neck. "They're hazel, kind of a yellowish brown. But sometimes, like when you tug on my heartstrings, they turn green."

"Earth tones," Josh softly repeated.

For an eternity of seconds, two pair of eyes were meshed in a rhapsody of longing. Josh would have remained in that moment forever, but Sarah had to push on. She turned on the tape recorder and spurred, "Where did you boys go after you left Eddie's Place, after that last slice of pumpkin pie?"

Josh flinched at the sound of the recorder-on key and abstained, "I don't want to talk about that today. What's your favorite movie?"

As much as Sarah hated the idea, she had to use Josh's obvious affection for her against him. "Josh! We don't have many more todays. If you want any more tomorrows looking at these hazel eyes, you'd better start talking. Where did you go after Thanksgiving?"

Josh was powerless in refusing Sarah's impassioned demand. "Your eyes are green now, Sarah."

So, Josh began to articulate his last memories of Ben. His syllables were more sobs than words. The only thing that kept him grinding out his story was that pair of green eyes.

Sarah listened to what she didn't want to hear but had to know. Later, wrapped in a comforter to warm her chills, she wrote the words that kept those hazel eyes green.

Session 4
9:05 am, September 21, 2001

The boys zig-zagged around the country with fifteen states to go. Sometimes, they found a load that was just too good to pass up, even though it took them back to a state they had just left. Sometimes, they accepted a load just because it took them to a state they had never seen.

Ben added to his number of friends in each state. It could be the guy next to him at the lunch counter. Within ten minutes, Ben would know his name, where he was from, and how many people were in his family. State-by-state, Ben found more good than evil in his world.

But Ben always kept track of the most evil deeds he could imagine. He had names and license plate numbers for every missing child clipped on the sun visor in the truck. He was always on the look-out, and if he could ever spot one of those license plate numbers, he would know what he was fighting for.

Josh didn't have Ben's unfailing faith that life would be more than this. His only desire was to get Ben to that fiftieth state.

It was in Tuscaloosa, Alabama, that Ben pasted the forty-eighth sticker on the back of the truck, and he sang, "Sweet Home Alabama."

Josh laughed and clapped in joy and amazement. They were less than four hours away from the forty-ninth state. Josh had stashed money away for many months. It was money Ben didn't know about. As soon as they dropped off their load in Georgia, Josh was going to buy airplane tickets to Hawaii, the fiftieth state.

Josh topped off the fuel tanks, and Ben made sure the windshield was perfectly clean and clear. They were embarking on the last leg of Josh's mission to show Ben all forty-nine states and then fly away to the fiftieth.

Ben could not sit still, and Josh could not stop laughing. "There it is, Josh, Interstate 20 East! Take this exit."

Josh knew how to keep those eighteen wheels turning, and Ben knew his maps. Ben was in charge now, and Josh would turn wherever Ben wanted.

"I 459 North, Josh!"

"North?" Josh questioned.

"Yeah, Josh, we'll turn back east in just a few miles," Ben assured.

After twenty more miles, Ben was ecstatic. "US 280 East! Turn here, Josh."

Josh gave a blast of the horn and declared at the top of his lungs, "YOU'RE THE MAN, BEN!"

A couple miles before Phenix City, Alabama, Ben was educating Josh. "Josh, it says here that we're going to be crossing the Chattahoochee River on the Dillingham Street Bridge, and – and on the other side of the bridge is Columbus, Georgia."

"And what should our next sticker say, Ben?"

Josh lit the last cigarette he would ever have and grinned in ultimate contentment as Ben poured through his books and maps and atlases. Today was a good day, and it held a promise of getting still better. Ben was happy, and that's all that mattered.

Ben jubilantly announced, "THE PEACH STATE!"

Josh choked with laughter on the last drag he would ever take off a cigarette. Then, that magnificent bridge appeared over the horizon. It was a long-revered marvel of architecture that had withstood ninety years of weather. Its low, concrete railings allowed the boys to see the grandeur of the Chattahoochee.

Half-way across the bridge, Josh had to slow to a stop. A vehicle was blocking the lane, while the driver scrambled to change the flat tire. Josh turned the emergency flashers on and looked at Ben. "Well, Ben – Ben?"

Ben was gasping short, quick breaths. "Jo – Josh. Dar–dark blue–Ford–Ford–Ranger. Melin–da."

Josh reached around for Ben's bag of pills, but Ben grabbed his head and turned it toward the pickup. Yes, it was a dark blue Ford Ranger, but Josh noted immediately, "That's a Georgia license plate, Ben. You've been looking for a Texas plate."

Josh looked back into the bag of pills, but Ben spun his head back around again. "LOOK! Bum–per–stick-stick-sticker."

Josh dropped the bag of pills, and a cold shudder went down his spine. The bumper sticker read, "Don't Mess with Texas."

Josh placed a hand behind Ben's head and drew their foreheads together. "Hold your breath, Ben."

The boys held their breath together, then breathed together until Ben could speak. No pill was necessary. Ben willed himself to demand, "We have to do something, Josh!"

Josh looked at the eastbound traffic stacking up behind the truck and then looked back to the man putting the lug nuts back on the left, front wheel. "I'll go check it out, Ben, but you stay in the truck. You hear me, Ben?"

Ben nodded his compliance, and Josh climbed down from the truck. He dodged the westbound traffic and made his way to the man who was tightening the last lug nut.

"I don't need no help," was the surly greeting Josh received.

Josh looked in the car and saw the young girl with blonde hair, which had been too long without a mother's care. He couldn't miss seeing the bruises on her arms and the fear in her eyes. "Melinda?" Josh chanced.

The young girl whimpered a shrill cry and Josh felt the steel of a snub-nose .38 pistol against his head. Josh raised his hands and froze. "Take it easy, man! I'll just…"

"You'll just get back in your truck," was the threatening order Josh received.

Before Josh could say another word, Ben appeared on the passenger side of the car. He yanked the passenger door open and called out, "MELINDA MILES!"

The snub-nose .38 was instinctively pointed at Ben, and the trigger was pulled. The bullet sliced through Ben's ear and he stumbled back. Ben could not comprehend what had just happened, he just kept stepping back until the low bridge railing took his legs out from under him, and Ben tumbled out of sight.

With no forethought or hesitation, Josh reacted with the involuntary reflex to run. He dove over the railing and watched his brother splash into the Chattahoochee. Josh pointed his hands toward the splash and locked his body straight as an arrow. As perfect as Josh's entry into the water was, the water resisted and stunned Josh into near unconsciousness.

Josh floated to the surface and gasped, "LORD, HELP ME!" Josh swam with the current, knowing nothing else to do. He swam, and he prayed. He swam, and he yelled, "BEN!"

It was over a mile down river when Josh caught up to Ben. Josh fought against the current for another mile before he got Ben to shore on the Georgia bank of the Chattahoochee, the 49th state.

No mortal breath could revive Ben. The only thing Josh's breath could do was SCREAM! He cried to God for help, and his howling split the air and echoed down the Chattahoochee.

Rescuers found the boys, nestled together in a fetal position. It was impossible for the naked eye to distinguish which, if either, was still alive. One had no pulse, and the other had a heart that no longer wished to beat.

Separating the two took an hour of delicate coaxing and gentle persuasion. When Josh finally let go of Ben, half a person walked away, and the other half was carried away.

Chapter 12

All that pain and suffering was indelibly captured on Sarah's tape recorder. The details would await the grace of Sarah's pen and paper and would play over and over in her heart and mind.

Sarah was permitted to accompany Josh back to his cell after he had poured out all his despair and misery. The two officers walked quietly behind, allowing Sarah to guide Josh gently by the arm. The officers could see that there was no fight left in this once fearless man.

The shoulders that had borne the weight of the world were now slumped and lifeless. The feet and legs that had always been ready to take a fighting stance were wobbly and unsure. This was a once proud young man whose only reason to live wouldn't let go of his arm.

Visiting hours were not applied to Sarah. Josh was displaying the classic signs that might have prompted a suicide watch, but no one could provide more comfort and ensure Josh's safety better than this incomparable young woman.

There were few words spoken for the next two hours, and no smiles exchanged. Through the cell bars, Sarah held Josh's right hand, and Josh held Sarah's left. The two bonded hearts mourned and prayed and loved. There was nothing else they could do. Life was what it had been and what it could be, if only…

"You go home, Sarah, and get some sleep," Josh suggested. "I'll be ok."

"I'll make you a deal, Josh," Sarah bargained. "I'll go home as soon as you go to sleep."

Josh didn't attempt to argue with this indomitable spirit. He let her fingers achingly slip away and laid on the bunk without losing sight of that slight frame clinging to the bars.

"Close your eyes, Josh, and listen."

Josh yielded to her bidding and Sarah sang,

"When you're down and out,
When you're on the street,
When evening falls so hard,
I will comfort you.
I'll take your part, oh, when darkness comes,
And pain is all, is all around,
Like a bridge over troubled water,
I will lay me down."

Sarah sang the whole song, and Josh heard part of it in his consciousness and the rest in his dreams. Even the officer standing guard in the cell block had to wipe his eyes on his sleeve.

Sarah could tell that Josh had fallen asleep by the evenness of his breathing and the occasional twitch of a dream. She wanted to stay all night, but she went home as promised.

She couldn't sleep, and she couldn't write the story that was still burning in her soul. She let the tears flow, hoping she would rid them from her eyes before she saw Josh again.

Alcohol was of no interest. Sleep was not possible. Nothing was imaginable without the soulmate she had left twitching on his bunk.

Sarah went for a drive without a destination. She took the backroads where headlights and street signs were few and far between. She drove all night until the sun came peeking over the horizon. Then, she parked.

At 9 am sharp, someone was parked in Phillip McCay's space when he arrived at work. He grumbled as he shifted the transmission into reverse and backed into space at the rear of the parking lot. He mouthed the words he had planned for this inconsiderate imbecile who had infringed on his daily routine.

He was jotting down the license plate number of this intruder when he noticed a young woman slumped over the steering wheel in a deflated heap. Her tangled hair concealed her face from the morning light.

McCay tapped on the driver's window, and Sarah jolted upright. The fear was evident in her eyes and in her trembling hand that rolled down the window. "Oh, Uncle Phil," Sarah sobbed.

Uncle Phil opened the car door, and Sarah clutched her satchel to her chest. Phil half-carried his niece into his office and sat her in the over-stuffed chair. He smoothed her hair away from her face and called to his intensely compassionate secretary. "Amanda, would you please get Sarah a cup of hot tea?"

Uncle Phil handed a box of tissues to Sarah, and Sarah exchanged it for the tape recording she couldn't bear to listen to again. Uncle Phil plugged the earpiece in and listened, while Sarah buried her face in handfuls of tissue.

Uncle Phil listened, and Sarah trembled until her hot tea splashed on her blouse. Amanda took the cup away from those shivering hands. "Let's go get you cleaned up, Missy."

Sarah went willingly as Amanda ushered her to the ladies' room. They first stood looking at each other in the mirror. It's sometimes easier not having to look someone straight in the eye. "Who is this guy?" Amanda delved.

Sarah dodged the question. "He's a client of Uncle Phil's, and he's a patient of mine."

Amanda knew that was not the whole story behind those tears that wouldn't stop, and she wagered, "Really nice guy, huh?"

Sarah couldn't hide behind her blotchy mascara and gave a quick nod.

"Better looking than most?" Amanda presumed.

Sarah's mouth pinched into a faint, but irrepressible smile and she nodded again.

Amanda put the lid down on the toilet and coaxed Sarah to sit. She then leaned back against the marble countertop with her hands resting on the marble, in her most open stance. "Tell me about this guy."

Amanda listened to the yearnings of a near-bursting heart. Sarah cupped her face in her hands, but her love spilled out like words spill out of an open book.

Amanda felt every tear and embraced every longing she heard. She took two strides to kneel in front of Sarah. "You're in love, girl. Do you know that?"

Sarah answered, with her whole body bobbing in admission. "I can't help it!"

Amanda remained on her knees, while her young ward cried herself into exhaustion. That's what Sarah needed, genuine understanding of how much love can hurt, empathetic sharing of all the feelings that consumed every fiber of her being. It was the better part of an hour before Sarah was ready to be escorted back to Uncle Phil's office.

Uncle Phil was looking out the expansive window and pacing in thought.

"Uncle Phil, do you think the man Josh killed was his brother's killer?" Sarah fearfully advanced.

Uncle Phil gestured his acknowledgment of the theory he could not dismiss. "If that's so, the prosecution will argue motive and premeditation."

"But, could you argue justifiable homicide?" Sarah groped.

"No," Uncle Phil regretted, "trying to establish justification would be seen by the jury only as a reason for revenge."

"But Josh wouldn't hurt anyone without a good reason," Sarah unquestionably declared. "What about self-defense?"

"He couldn't defend his brother anymore," Uncle Phil pointed out, "and I'm pretty sure Josh is capable of defending himself without killing. Then, there's the matter of the gun. There were .38 caliber slugs found in the wall and the attic. But, there was no gun at the crime scene. The presumption is that it was Josh's gun, and if so, it would tend to further support premeditation."

Uncle Phil turned and observed that Sarah was ready to fall apart again. He walked toward her dejected slouch, knelt down, and lifted her chin, just as he had done for her skinned knees and bruised elbows. "However, self-defense extends to the protection of anyone – like maybe a young girl wrapped in a blanket."

"Melinda Miles!" Sarah shouted.

"Look, Sarah," Uncle Phil admonished, "we can't withhold this information much longer. The prosecution will eventually identify Josh, and that will lead them to identifying the victim."

"I wish you would stop calling him the victim," Sarah objected. "Ben was the victim. Melinda was the victim. Even – even Josh is still a victim."

"And that's what we're going to make a jury believe," Uncle Phil assured. "But we need to stay a couple steps ahead of the prosecution, so we have a few ducks to get in a row."

"What do we do, Uncle Phil?"

Uncle Phil sat on the floor with his legs crossed and invited Sarah to join him. They sat cross-legged, with their foreheads mere inches apart, as if they were planning their next daring adventure in Sarah's childhood.

"You go home and get yourself presentable to talk some more with Josh," Uncle Phil instructed. "I have his parents flying in tomorrow, and we'll meet them at the airport."

Sarah could not contain herself and lunged forward to hug her Uncle's neck. She hugged like the time her prince saved her from their imaginary dragon. That was the response Uncle Phil had been hoping for.

"That's my girl," Uncle Phil chuckled. "For the rest of today, I'm going to be looking for Melinda Miles. And you're going to be extracting every detail you can from that young man, so we can get his ass out of jail. Are you ready for the quest, my fair young Princess?"

"Lead the way my gallant Prince," Sarah swore. "And I will follow."

Uncle Phil helped his beautiful princess to her feet, reached to square her shoulders, turned her to face the door, and ordered, "March!"

Sarah marched in exaggerated steps and stopped at the door to blow her handsome prince a kiss. Her prince captured her kiss in his palm, planted it on his cheek, and bowed in utter adoration of his princess' unwavering devotion.

Sarah drove home and headed straight for the shower. She washed the tangles out of her hair and scrubbed her fears down the drain. She didn't touch her make-up. She didn't brighten her eyes or gloss her lips. She was going to confront Josh in the raw beauty of the love that she had professed.

She stood in the hallway of the police station, watching Josh approach. There was only one officer, keeping a light grip on his arm. Josh had regained some semblance of composure and no longer presented a threat. But Sarah could see the gloomy helplessness in those once fiery eyes.

She sat across the table and waited for Josh's eyes to find the courage to look at her. "How are you doing, Sweetheart?" Sarah slipped.

"Sweetheart?" Josh's ears could not miss.

"OH! I'm sorry," Sarah tried to retract. But Sarah's heartfelt blunder could not be disguised.

"That's ok," Josh encouraged. "I really like the sound of that."

Sarah tried to regroup. "No, we need to stick with Josh and Sarah."

Josh didn't make it easy on her. "I like the sound of that even more, "Josh and Sarah."

Sarah couldn't speak it, but her eyes could not deny it. "I do too." She squinted her eyes to conceal the love spilling out and sternly set her jaw.

Josh was now facing a woman of purpose and determination. He had seen that look in his mother's face. This was a woman who meant business.

Josh tried to diffuse and distract. "Your hair smells great, Sarah."

"That's just shampoo, Josh," Sarah dismissed.

Josh shuffled and fidgeted, trying to avoid the questions he knew Sarah would ask. "Did you have a nice evening last night?"

Sarah maintained the upper hand and wielded it in relentless resolve. "I'm here to talk about you, Josh."

Josh shriveled and looked away. "We've talked enough about me."

"No, Josh, we haven't. You haven't told me what happened after Ben died."

Josh bolted out of his chair and turned to look out the window at the officer posted outside. The officer could see the anguish in Josh's face, and though he couldn't hear the words, he felt the pain.

"There is no more story after Ben! There will never be a...!"

"Josh!" Sarah commanded.

"Josh," Sarah tried to persuade.

Josh could not resist the need to turn and face Sarah.

Sarah glided across the room and lifted Josh's chin. She locked his face in her hands, and there was no escape for Josh. Her voice was firm, but her words were nothing but love. "There is a story after Ben. There's a story about Jake and Cassie Marshall, who lost a son and need to hear what happened to the other son."

Josh's body went limp. He sank to the floor, and Sarah moved her hand from his face to his heart. She looked at the officers on the other side of the windows, in an appeal for humanity. The officers turned about and faced away.

Sarah held Josh's head and laid her face in his hair. Josh sputtered and choked out the words, and Sarah listened. Sarah took no notes that day, and she never got the tape recorder turned on. She didn't have to. Josh's story was unerasably etched in her heart until she was alone with her pen, her paper, her tears, and her Chablis.

Chapter 13

Not a word or a feeling left Sarah's mind until it streamed onto the page. Josh's story was no longer his alone. Sarah had a stake in every tear that flowed from her pen. Her next chapter of Josh's story was even harder than the last.

Session 5
9:10 am, September 22, 2001

Josh didn't remember much about the next three days after he lost Ben. He remembered a deluge of questions from authorities, but no answers. There was no sign of Melinda Miles or her captor. The police sketch artist matched Melinda's face from the details imprinted in Josh's mind. But the face of the man who sent Ben to his death was a blur of evil.

Momma and Daddy came to take Josh home, but they feared they had lost both sons. One would be laid to rest, and the other seemed to be teetering on the precipice of hell.

Josh remembered waking in the upper bunk, where he had slept a childhood. But the lower bunk was empty. Josh came racing down the stairs, and his screams woke a household. "BEN! WHERE'S BEN?"

Jake caught his son at the bottom of the stairs, and the two fell to the floor. Cassie was right behind and dropped to the floor to cradle her boy. Jake and Cassie held fast to the flailing body of their son, who could still not grasp or accept the loss of his biggest reason for taking another breath.

No words could explain the reason, and even Gretchen's prayers could not ease the pain. Scores of vets came for Ben's funeral. Ben had lit all their lives, and he was their hero. But all the pain they shared could not subtract from the torment that Josh bore.

Josh no longer found joy in fishing with his Daddy, because Ben was not there. His Momma's love was poured out on him, but Josh didn't know how to embrace it without sharing it with Ben. Josh tried to work on the farm to make himself forget, but the harder he worked, the more he realized that he didn't want to forget.

He had to finish Ben's dream. That dream was all he had left of Ben. He had to find the young girl, whose name was the last words he heard Ben speak. He was going to tell that girl about the boy who loved her for thousands of miles. He was going to tell her about the man who looked for her in fifteen states.

Josh stayed in constant contact with the Columbus Police Department and begged for information about Melinda Miles. But the police were not one step closer to finding her, and each week that passed made Ben's death more futile. If Josh could do only one more thing on this earth, he was going to find Melinda Miles.

Josh packed his bag and left a note. He had a new purpose in life, and his note described it the best he could.

Dear Momma and Daddy,

"I'm sorry I didn't hug you goodbye. Ben would have, but I'm not Ben. And I don't know who I am without him.

Did you ever notice that I hardly ever looked in a mirror? I didn't have to. I just looked at Ben. He told me whether my hair was combed or if I needed to wipe the soup off my chin.

I never cried when Ben was around. He cried for me. And I laughed only when I saw his goofy grin. I've learned to cry now, but I don't know if I'll ever laugh again.

I know that Ben is in the bosom of Our Lord, but I don't understand everything Gretchen tells me about Heaven. How can Ben be at peace when the last thing his heart desired still needs to be done?

I'll write to you, Momma. And, Daddy, I don't know when, but someday I will find my way home.

LOVE,

Your Son, and My Brother's Keeper

Josh left before the rooster crowed. He watched everything he held dear disappear in the rear-view mirror. Then, he fixed his eyes toward the southeast and set his course for the Dillingham Street Bridge. That was where life as he knew it had ended, and that was where his quest would begin.

Josh was drawn to the sight where his brother left his life like a moth is drawn to the light. He stood at the exact point where Ben had taken his last stand. He shouted down the Chattahoochee that had claimed Ben's last breath. "BEN! WE WILL FIND MELINDA, YOU AND ME! But I can't do it alone, Brother. I need your help. Tell me where to look, and I will seek. Tell me when to breathe, and I will spend my last breath getting Melinda back home."

After Josh had given his solemn oath to the memory of Ben, he headed east. When he arrived in Columbus, Georgia, the police still had nothing to tell him and no plan to carry the search forward. But Josh had a plan.

He armed himself with ample copies of the police sketch of evil and photos of Melinda Miles. His plan was simple, just as Ben would have suggested. Josh would search every highway, street, and parking lot. It didn't matter how long it would take, nothing on this earth would keep him from fulfilling his pledge to his brother.

Josh drove all day every day. He stopped and searched every bar, gas station, and grocery store in Columbus. Some days he ate. Some days he didn't. Somedays he slept and some nights he couldn't.

He didn't keep track of the money he had spent or the miles he had driven. The only thing his mind could retain was Ben's words, "We have to find her, Josh."

Josh searched until his money was half gone. Then, he got a job here and a job there. Anything requiring a strong back and a dulled mind was not beneath him. He worked as many hours as necessary for a full day's pay, so long as he had a few hours left in the day to search.

Josh wrote many letters home, but few of them were mailed. He poured his heart into each letter, but the only thoughts he would allow his Momma and Daddy to read spoke of how he was eating right and praying right.

Josh wrote other letters too. He wrote to Ben every night, telling him about the roads he had traveled and the people he had met. None of those letters were mailed, but each one was delivered. They were delivered by the current of the Chattahoochee River.

The last job Josh held was at a gas station convenience store, less than a mile east of the Dillingham Street Bridge. The owner of the store was a small man in his late 50's. Josh guessed that he might be Southeast Asian from his accent and his gentle features. His face held a history of war and peace. Josh felt an instant bond when their eyes first met.

Josh was hired after a very brief interview. The owner had only one question to ask. "Is your father well?"

"Yes, Sir," was Josh's baffled answer. "Thank you for asking, Mr. Nguyen. Did you know my father?"

Mr. Nguyen reached out and laid his hand over Josh's heart. "Let me show you how cash register work."

There was something more going on as Mr. Nguyen taught Josh which buttons to push on the cash register. He was nurturing a young man that had immediately *found a special place in his heart. Josh could see it in the crinkle of the old man's eyes. He could hear it in the soft tones of the old man's voice.*

Josh had to know more about this man who treated him like an adopted son. "Mr. Nguyen, is that a Vietnamese name?"

The old man answered with more of a bow than a nod. "Yes, young Josh. Let me show you where mop and broom are."

Josh swept and mopped and straightened the goods on the shelves. All the while, he kept an eye on the old man's smile. It was a smile of contentment and peace that Josh wished he could possess.

Josh had put in more than a day's work when he locked the door and turned down the lights. The old man was taking the left-over burritos and corn dogs out of the warmer and wrapping them in foil. He handed Josh a hearty meal and his heartfelt thanks. "Thank you, Young Josh. You work hard. Now, you eat good."

"Thank you, Mr. Nguyen. I appreciate that – and – uh – Mr. Nguyen?"

"Yes, young Josh, you may have a drink from the cooler. Anything you want." The old man turned to place the tongs in the sink to be washed.

"No, Mr. Nguyen, - I mean – I have to ask you something." The old man paused, sensing what might come next.

Josh apprehensively divulged, "My father was a prisoner of war in Vietnam."

The tongs clinked and pinged against the other utensils in the sink, and the old man froze.

Josh proceeded in hopeful disbelief. "My father spoke of only one Vietnamese soldier."

The old man turned away and began to close out the daily receipts in the cash register.

Josh persisted in his query that had to be answered. "He spoke of a young North Vietnamese soldier – a boy, really, who helped him escape. Without the help of that young soldier, I would not be here today."

The old man opened the cash drawer, and Josh watched his hands tremble as he counted the cash and coin.

"Mr. Nguyen?" Josh entreated. The old man paused, with a handful of quarters clenched in his fist.

Josh took the chance of speaking one more time. "That young Vietnamese soldier was named Hi-Hi."

The handful of quarters fell and clattered on the floor. The old man sank to his knees, and a tear streamed down each cheek. He started to pick up the quarters one-by-one as if he was counting memories.

Josh knelt and waited until the old man raised his head. Josh saw the compassion in those eyes that his father had seen so many years ago, and Hi-Hi saw the hope that he had seen in the eyes of Josh's father.

"Mr. Nguyen, did you know my father? Is your name Hi-Hi?"

Hi-Hi's head fell forward, and he acknowledged, "You have your father's eyes. I never forget eyes."

"Oh, Mr. Nguyen!" Josh erupted. "You have been my hero since I was a little boy."

The old man sat back and shook his head in disagreement. "Not hero. Just scared young boy." The old man feigned a smile and suggested, "Get us a beer, young Josh."

Josh and his hero sat on the floor with quarters strewn around and shared corn dogs, burritos, and beer.

"Your father a very brave man. He was our prisoner, but he was not my enemy." Hi-Hi washed down a bite of corn dog and remembered. "They treat him bad, and I cry for him. Your father try to fight, but – they hurt him more."

Josh was downing his beer faster than Hi-Hi, trying to wash down the lump in his throat. Hi-Hi swished his corn dog like a knife through the air. "SO, I CUT HIM LOOSE!"

The broadest of smile overtook Hi-Hi's face. "He run one way, and I run another. I was running away. Your father was running "to." Hi-Hi pointed his corn dog right at Josh's nose. "To you."

Hi-Hi balanced his empty bottle upside-down on the floor. "Get us another beer, young Josh, and tell me about your family."

Josh and Hi-Hi toasted a friendship that had begun before Josh was born. Josh began picking up quarters, memory by memory. Hi-Hi listened behind closed eyelids and met Grandma and Grandpa, Auntie Jo and Josh's beautiful mother, Cassie. He chuckled at each story of sister, Gretchen, and brother, Ben.

Josh balanced his second bottle, upside-down on the floor. All the quarters had been counted, but all the memories had not. Josh recounted his last days with Ben and his days without him. Hi-Hi cringed and wept while Josh described the last day of Ben's life, and the story of Melinda Miles.

"That's why I'm here, Mr. Nguyen." Josh reached in his pocket and unfolded the picture of Melinda Miles.

Hi-Hi stroked the delicate features in the photo with a gentle finger. "Beautiful young girl. How old is she?"

"She's twelve, Mr. Nguyen."

"How long she gone?"

"About nine months. I've been looking for her for five months."

Mr. Nguyen bowed and wagged his head and decided he didn't want the rest of his beer.

"I've looked everywhere, Mr. Nguyen, here in Columbus and over in Phenix City." Josh reached in his pocket again. "Here's a sketch of the man who's holding her captive."

Mr. Nguyen's eyes widened in slow but sure recognition. He rose to his knees and bellowed, "I SEE THIS MAN! ONE WEEK AGO!"

Josh leapt to his feet and grabbed the old man by the shoulders. "Are you sure, Mr. Nguyen?"

"I never forget eyes," the old man assured. "He buy gas and coffee and candy."

Josh held up Melinda's picture and pushed for more information. "Was this girl with him?"

"There was young girl in car. I don't see her face, but she have blonde hair like this girl."

The old man banged every memory out of his head. "I ask this man where he going. He say back to God's country, Plano."

"PLANO?" Josh was gyrating into a frenzy. "That's just outside of Dallas, where she first went missing!"

Josh appealed for any information he could get. "Please, Mr. Nguyen, what kind of car was he driving?"

The old man held his head and tried to thump something helpful out of it. "Don't know what kind – small car – white." His eyes flashed as he recalled something of use. "Right side door – BLUE!"

Josh sailed over the counter and sped out into the parking lot. As he cranked up his car, he saw the old man standing at pump #3 with the gas nozzle in his hand. Josh pulled up to the pump, and the old man began to dispense all the fuel the tank would hold.

The old man reached through the car window to grasp Josh's hand. "Young Josh, never run from. Just like your father, always run "to."

Josh leapt out of the car and held the old man in an embrace that was far more than anything he could say. The compassion of a young boy soldier and the generosity of an old man named Hi-Hi had transcended a generation. Josh planted a kiss next to the old man's ear and dove back behind the steering wheel.

The old man replaced the nozzle on pump #3 and watched young Josh speed west. He pulled out his handkerchief as he ambled back to the store. After he locked the front door, he daubed a tear and swiped his nose. Then, he turned off the light.

Chapter 14

It was getting exceptionally late when Sarah printed the last page of her manuscript, documenting Josh's endeavors. Sleep was the next of her priorities, but she didn't know if that was possible. Then, the phone rang.

"Sarah, Josh's folks are due at the airport at 10:00 am, and I might be a little late getting back from Murphy," Uncle Phil announced.

"Murphy? What are you doing in Murphy, Uncle Phil?"

"I found Melinda, Honey. She's safe at home with her parents."

Sarah let loose with a scream that made Uncle Phil yank the phone receiver off his ear. He listened until the shriek turned into a giggle.

"Her parents don't want her to appear in court," Uncle Phil enlightened. "They wouldn't even let me talk with her. And, Honey, even if I could get a court subpoena, if you were that child, I wouldn't want you subpoenaed either. The family never knew Josh's name. He just delivered Melina home and took off. I left them a picture of Josh, hoping they have the courage and compassion to show it to the girl."

"Thank you, Uncle Phil. Thank you, my knight in shining armor!"

"Good night, my lady. I'll see you at the airport."

Sarah was at the police station earlier than she had ever been the next morning. Sleep was no longer the priority. She had to see Josh. It was breakfast time, and Sarah snatched Josh's tray out of the officer's hands. The officer threw his head back in an inward laugh and then opened the cellblock door.

Josh was still asleep on his bunk when Sarah asked, "Can I have a slice of your toast?"

Josh rolled and tumbled to the floor. He was flat on his back, watching Sarah sniff his breakfast. He turned on his side and doubled over in laughter that he had not felt since Supercalifragilisticexpialidocious. He climbed the cell bars hand-over-hand and pulled himself to his feet.

Sarah had a slice of toast clenched in her teeth and passed the tray through the slot in the bars. Josh took the tray and sniffed the food that now smelled better than anything he'd had since Mr. Nguyen's burritos and corn dogs.

"Anything I have is yours," Josh swore. "I just don't have anything," he roared.

"You've got me," Sarah blundered again. "I mean…" she stammered. "We're friends, right? I mean…" Sarah hid her face behind her hands and then dropped them to her sides, with the toast in one hand and with a stomp of her foot. "Will you just shut up and eat?"

Josh sat on his bunk and spoke with a mouthful of scrambled eggs. "Are we going to talk as soon as I finish this?" With two more quick bites, the eggs were gone.

"We're going to be delayed until this afternoon, Josh."

Josh stuffed both sausage links in his mouth and nodded with his whole body. He chewed quickly so he could swallow just enough to ask, "You have another appointment, huh?"

Sarah waited until Josh had downed the whole cup of milk. "I'm going to meet your parents, Josh." Sarah held her breath in anticipation of what she knew would happen.

Josh's tray clanged on the floor, and his cup rolled across the cell. Josh launched himself across the cell in one vaulting stride and gripped the bars. "Are they here?"

He didn't have the look of dread he had shown before. Sarah saw the excitement of a little boy who had lost his way, and now Mom and Dad had found him.

Sarah reached through the bars to glide her fingers from Josh's hair to his chin. "I'm meeting them at the airport in less than an hour, and I can't wait."

"Tell them – tell Mom and Dad…"

Sarah moved her fingers to silence Josh's lips. "You'll tell them, Hon." Sarah stomped her foot again at her misstep.

"I like Sweetheart better," Josh beseeched.

Sarah reached for Josh's hands, and he gladly gave them. "There's one more thing, Sweetheart," Sarah shared with no correction. "My Uncle found Melinda Miles, and she's doing fine."

Josh dropped to his knees and cried the tears that Ben wasn't there to shed. He cried for a young girl who had another shot at life. He cried for the sake of Ben's peace in Heaven. And he wept because maybe someday he could tell Gretchen what he was fighting for.

"I have to get to the airport, Hon – I mean, Sweetheart. Are you going to be ok?"

"Only when I see you again, My Love."

"My Love?" Sarah repeated over and over in her mind and giggled, "Now, I really like that."

Sarah's fingers slipped painfully out of Josh's grip until only their fingertips touched. The only way Sarah could leave was to turn and run.

The officer opened the cell block door, so as not to impede Sarah's stride. Her pace slowed only slightly for each turn, as she careened through the corridors and bounced off the walls to stay on her feet. People stepped out of her way and cheered her on. They didn't know where Sarah was going, but everyone in the police station knew that it had to do with the love they had seen between Josh and Sarah.

Sarah left her black rubber marks in the parking lot, when her tires screeched and spun, then gripped the pavement. Her heart was soaring, and her mind was racing, but the car was racing even faster. Stop signs were a nuisance that Sarah defied. She assumed at every turn that she had the right-of-way. No one had an appointment more important than hers.

The speed limit sign escaped Sarah's attention, but the short "Whoop" of the siren and the flashing of red and blue brought her back to earth. She pulled over and freaked when she looked at her watch that showed only twenty minutes to make a thirty-minute drive. She stuck her arm out the window and waved for the officer to hurry.

The officer picked up the pace and hustled to her open window. "Is something the matter, Ma'am?"

"Yes! I have to get to the airport."

The officer had heard that excuse countless times and resumed his protocol. "Yes, Ma'am. May I see your driver's license, registration, and proof of insurance?"

Sarah rummaged frantically through her purse until its contents fell on the passenger floorboard. On top of the heap was her driver's license and her wavering hand struggled to seize it and get it into the officer's hand. "OH! I'M SORRY, JOSH! OH, GOD! PLEASE HELP ME."

"Just calm down, Ma'am. Take a moment to relax."

Sarah pointed at her watch. "I don't have a moment! I have to meet Josh's parents."

The officer took a cursory look at Sarah's driver's license and asked, "Sarah Langston?"

It was difficult to distinguish Sarah's nod from the shaking of her entire body. "Please step out of the car, Ma'am."

Tears cascaded down Sarah's face as the officer extracted her keys from the ignition and locked the door. The officer took Sarah by the arm, led her to his patrol car, and opened the passenger door. "Please get in the car, Ma'am."

The officer ran to get behind the steering wheel and spoke over the siren and the rpm of the engine. "Josh and Sarah."

Sarah perked up her ears at the sound she most treasured. "That love story has been floating around the precinct for weeks," Officer Bounds shared. "Don't worry, Sarah, we'll make it."

Sarah's elation glowed as they sped to the airport. Motorists pulled to the side of the road and cleared the way for the most important engagement of her life. Perhaps the drivers yielding the right-of-way thought they were aiding in the saving of someone's life. They had no idea, but they would have been thrilled to know that they were part of making someone's dream come true.

Sarah had to wait until the patrol car stopped in the passenger drop-off zone before she wrapped her arms around Officer Bounds' neck. "Thank you. I owe you warm cookies, and I won't forget."

"Just go, girl. Go get 'em," Officer Bounds cheered.

A quick look at her watch showed Sarah there were two minutes to go. She took off her shoes and ran. She ran like a wide receiver, dodging tacklers and hurtling over luggage. Up the escalator and through the corridors she flew. Nothing could stop her until she rammed into that one immovable object. Sarah looked up and saw the fifty-some-year-old version of her sweetheart's face.

"Mr.–Mr.–Mar-shall!" she panted. Sarah hugged Jake's neck like she wasn't allowed to hug Josh's.

Jake lifted her off her feet and carried her to a chair. Cassie helped lower Sarah into the seat and cooed, "You must be Sarah."

Jake studied Sarah's green eyes and then looked at Cassie's. "Yep, those are eyes our boy would fall for. Sarah, your Uncle, told us about you and what you've been doing for Josh. How is our boy?"

"He can't wait to see you!" Sarah buzzed in exhilaration. "But – I have to tell you it took weeks for him to get over his fear of facing you."

"But he's always been able to come to us when he was in trouble," Jake asserted.

"This is different, Mr. Marshall. Jake has had a very traumatic experience," Sarah explained. "He didn't know how to tell you, and he's still not ready to talk about everything. He was willing to rot in jail rather than involve you folks."

"He's always been that way," Jake remembered. "He wanted to handle everything on his own."

Cassie chimed in, "I don't know how many times he took the blame for anything he or his brother did, regardless of the consequences."

Sarah removed her manuscript from its case and held it in her lap. "I've written everything Josh has told me. We started at the beginning when the boys were on the road. He talked about Thanksgiving and the note he left you. He told me about – Ben – and – the bridge." Sarah's words were squealing and shaking out of her.

Cassie put her motherly arm around Sarah. "We know all about that, Dear. We need to know what happened after he left home."

Sarah thumbed through the pages at a feverish pace, knowing where every word was. "Here, start here."

"Jake, I think we need coffee," Cassie recommended.

The three allied companions, bonded through one remarkable young man, found a small bistro table, and Jake went to order coffee. Cassie tapped the ends of the unbound pages on the table to square them up and began reading. She had finished the first two pages when Jake returned with piping hot comfort. She passed the two pages to Jake and continued to stay a page or two ahead of him.

Sarah watched their brows furl and their lips purse. She squirmed in her chair as each page was turned. Near the end of the fourth page, Cassie discovered the name, Hi-Hi. Her back stiffened, and her eyes clamped shut.

"Cassie?" Jake urged with his hand held out for the next page.

Cassie scooted out of her chair and stood behind Jake. She laid the remaining pages in front of him and wrapped her arms around his neck. They read together, with their heads inseparable. "That young Vietnamese soldier was named Hi-Hi," Jake gasped aloud. Jake and Cassie swayed and rocked together, reciting in unison. "Mr. Nguyen, you've been my hero since I was a little boy."

They read the pages again, each with only one hand free of the other's hair. Sarah sipped her coffee and watched the brows relax and the lips part in waning disbelief.

Jake and Cassie learned what they had wanted to know for many months. They discovered what their boy had been up to. It was not surprising to read about the noble quest their boy had claimed. Every word was believable because they knew their son. Every ounce of love in those words was what they already knew.

Phillip McCay approached and joined the group. He put his left hand on Sarah's shoulder and reached out with his right. "Mr. Marshall, I'm Phillip McCay."

McCay's handshake was firm and sure. That had always been Jake's surest way of measuring up a man. "Thank you for calling us Mr. McCay. I am forever in your debt. How serious are the charges against our boy, Mr. McCay?" Jake boldly inquired.

"I think you should call me Phil." Phil nodded to Cassie. "Mrs. Marshall."

Cassie offered her hand and reciprocated, "And we are Jake and Cassie."

"Of course, any murder charge is a serious matter," Phil answered.

"Our boy is not a murderer," Jake demanded. "I need to hear what Josh has to say."

Phil raised and lowered his hand in a gesture suggesting silence. Other bistro patrons were casting looks of shock and intrigue. "We need to go somewhere a bit more private."

Everyone carried a piece of luggage. Everyone bore their share of the burden that comes with love. All the luggage fit in Uncle Phil's spacious trunk, but the car could barely contain all the tender feelings for one young man. The luxurious leather seats could not assuage all the anxiety that came with the caring and devotion to a guy named Josh.

Phil drove, Sarah rode shotgun, and Jake and Cassie clung to each other in the back seat. Jake remained silent as long as he could, but that was not long.

"I'm telling you, Phil, our boy, is a fighter when the chips are down, but he is not a murderer," Jake insisted again.

"I tend to agree folks," Phil concurred. "It's difficult to imagine a hero like Josh being a murderer."

"Hero?" Jake and Cassie echoed.

Phil tilted his head back with a smile of admiration. "Tell them, Sarah."

Sarah turned to face the back, "Josh got Melinda Miles home safely."

Jake and Cassie's faces were illuminated with pride and overwhelmed by joy. They exchanged an incredulous look between them and Cassie moaned softly, "He promised Ben he would."

There was no longer a question of what their boy had been up to. He had been chasing his brother's dream, and he had found the last desire his brother had lived for and died for.

Phil pulled up in front of a supper club where the sign said closed. He got out of the car and strolled to the front door. His knock was answered, and he requested, "Stanley, I need a booth and some privacy to conduct some business."

Phil and Stanley ushered the group in, and they were seated with Stanley's renowned hospitality. "May I get you all something to drink?"

"I'll have my single malt, Stanley," Phil replied. "What would everyone else like?"

"Just water, thank you," Jake requested. "Me too," Cassie agreed. Sarah would have liked something a little stiffer, but she followed suit with Mom and Dad. "Water would be fine, thank you. Maybe with a slice of lemon?"

Stanley bowed in his professional servitude and left to prepare the refreshments. Jake anxiously pushed, "How do we get my boy out of jail?"

Phil waved his hand in consolation and patience. "Please wait a few more moments, Jake. My words are only for you and Cassie."

Stanley delivered the glasses, and Phil handed him a large bill of gratitude. He waited until Stanley retired to his duties in the back room and proceeded. "Jake, Cassie, the prosecution has been gathering evidence, some pretty flimsy, and some rather troubling. And, there's something you need to know."

Phil leaned back, dreading what he had to say next. "Josh has confided to Sarah and myself only, that he did kill the man that is referred to as the murder victim."

Half of Jake's water sloshed across the table, and Cassie's glass fell to the floor. They were both speechless and huddled together in helplessness.

Stanley poked his head out from the back room, and Phil waved him away. Stanley closed the door with a perceptive nod, and Phil continued.

"The police have eyewitnesses, and some weak forensic evidence that suggests that Josh may have been at the scene of the crime."

Cassie buried her face in her hands, and Jake set his jaw against a scream.

Phil hastened to assure, "They have no reliable evidence of guilt - yet. But, I suspect they will have soon. The photograph of the murder victim closely matches the police sketch Josh described as the man who killed your son, Ben."

Jake shoved the table out of his way and stood to bellow, "THEN YOU TELL THE JUDGE AND JURY THAT MAN NEEDED TO BE KILLED!"

Phil hung his head in quiet empathy and waited until Cassie and Sarah could persuade Jake to sit again. It wasn't easy for them. Jake struggled and resisted, but then, submitted to the four arms wrapped around him.

"I need to mount a defense that is acceptable under the law, Jake," Phil advised.

Jake nodded in reluctant acceptance.

"Our best shot is to enter a plea of self-defense," Phil counseled.

"I want to see Josh now," Jake pleaded with his head still bowed.

"You'll get to talk to him as soon as possible," Phil guaranteed. "But, when the police become aware of your presence, they're going to want to talk with you first."

Jake launched back onto the offensive. "I'm going to go see Josh now!" he swore.

"The police will not allow it, Jake," Phil informed. "They'll want to hear your statements before any possible conspiratory conversation between you and your son."

"Will you be there, Phil?" Cassie needed to hear.

"I'll be there every step of the way," Phil assured.

Jake thought about all the times he had helped his son and about all the times he couldn't. He thought about all the times he had to stand back and trust his son. He reached out with his calloused farmer's hand. "Take care of our boy, Phil. You lead, and we'll follow."

Chapter 15

Phil dropped Sarah off at her car and drove the Marshall's to the police station. Sarah made a U-turn in the most inhospitable traffic and pointed her car back to Josh.

Phil and the Marshall's arrived at the police station first, and Phil escorted them in an unassailable parade to Detective Hallstrom's office. Without invitation, he introduced them to the man whose job it was to put their son away, or possibly to death.

"Jake, Cassie, this is Detective Hallstrom," Phil acquainted. "Detective, this is Mr. and Mrs. Marshall. They are Josh's parents."

Hallstrom slowly rose from his chair, with his mouth agape. He extended his hand and Jake accepted it, only to measure up the man he was dealing with. It was not a friendly handshake. It was not the handshake of a man he would buy a used car from, and certainly not the handshake of a man he would entrust with the fate of his son.

Jake made his unretractable statement clear. "My son is not a murderer."

Hallstrom winced at the strength of Jake's grip and implored, "Please have a seat Mr. and Mrs. Marshall."

Cassie sat and tugged on the back pocket of Jake's jeans. Jake relaxed his grip and gradually descended into his chair. He maintained his glare, and Hallstrom knew that he was still in the crosshairs of Jake's sights.

"Mr. and Mrs. Marshall, I hold no ill will toward your son," Hallstrom tried to diffuse. "But I have to exhaust every effort in this investigation. Would you please tell me when you last saw Josh?"

Cassie took control of the conversation, while Jake kept a vigilant surveillance on Hallstrom's intent. "It was five months ago," Cassie disclosed.

Hallstrom averted his eyes from Jake's ominous snarl of a gaze and concentrated on Cassie. "What, would you say, was the state of his mind when you last saw him? Was he depressed, angry, perhaps vengeful?"

Jake's snarl was now audible, but Cassie kept the lead. "Yes, all of those. But mostly, just – heartbroken."

Cassie wringed her hands and took a few labored breaths. "I don't know if you can imagine, Detective. I don't even know if I can. What is it like to lose the one person who defined you since birth? What is it like to take half a breath and not be able to let it out? How do you go on after your heart has been ripped from your chest?"

Cassie took those half breaths and fought to exhale, as one does with a paper bag over their face, trying to conquer their hyperventilation. Phil tried to rescue Cassie and Jake through authoritative confrontation. "I think that the Marshalls have given you all the information they can. Jake and Cassie, would you please wait for me in the hall while I have a brief word with the Detective?"

"One more question, Counselor." Hallstrom took the chance of looking Jake head-on. "Could your son break a man's neck with his bare hands?"

Jake rose steadily and powerfully. He laid his hands on Hallstrom's desk and leaned within an inch of his nose. "It depends on whose neck it is."

Hallstrom nodded and gave a conciliatory grin. "I see where your son got his fighting spirit."

"NO! You don't see, Detective," Jake defied. "My son learned devotion to family from generations of Marshalls, but his fighting spirit came from hundreds of vets who were ready and willing to lay down their lives for a brother. Are you a veteran, Detective?"

"No, Sir, I am not, but I understand..." Hallstrom tried to deflect.

"NO, YOU DO NOT UNDERSTAND!" Jake thundered. "You cannot possibly understand unless you have held a dying brother in your arms. You will never understand why my son is a better man than you or I will ever be. You have my son locked up, BUT YOU WILL NOT DEFEAT HIM!"

Jake's rage was building, but it had not yet reached its pinnacle. Cassie took Jake by the hand and towed him out the door. Jake succumbed to Cassie's tug, but he was still shouting. "LET ME SEE MY SON!"

Jake and Cassie waited in the hall. Hallstrom watched Jake slam his fist against the wall, and Cassie stilled his rage with a touch of her hand. McCay watched and let the scene play out.

After a moment of silent retrospect, Hallstrom grabbed the first shot at spouting off his mouth to McCay. "I think I have my motive now."

McCay calmly countered, "You have nothing."

Hallstrom arrogantly proclaimed, "I have a suspect who was at the murder scene of the man who killed his brother." He paused to bask in his small victory, and then gloated, "How long did you think it would take me to discover that?"

McCay nodded in doubtful acquiescence. "So, do you have a name for your murder victim?"

"Well, no," Hallstrom faltered. "but he closely resembles the police sketch provided by your client."

McCay patronizingly responded, "Closely resembles – uh huh."

"Look, McCay," Hallstrom tried to dominate. "I have pieces of evidence that are starting to fit together. As soon as I get Melinda Miles to identify the victim..."

McCay cut Hallstrom's fantasy short. "Good luck with that, Detective."

McCay stepped out into the hall and put one arm around Cassie's shoulders and the other around Jake's. "Now, I get to do the second-best part of my job."

"What's the best part, Phil?" Cassie encouraged.

"When Josh is where I am right now," Phil revelled, "between you two."

Phil halted at the edge of the window, where Sarah and Josh could be seen hand-in-hand and nose-to-nose. "Take a peek," Phil entreated.

Jake and Cassie peered through the edge of the glass and watched a reflection of themselves thirty years ago. The love they saw was a love that had lived through generations. It was a love that had been taught. It was the love they had felt. It was the love they had passed on.

Jake bolted to the door. He swung the door wide, and his brawny frame filled the doorway. Josh glanced. Josh did a double-take. Josh RAN.

There were over two decades of love in Josh's hug. Two decades of trials, victories, and defeats melded into the only thing that matters, love. That hug could have lasted for hours. But then, there was the face of Momma. Josh lifted Cassie off her feet and spun around the room. Cassie felt the embrace of two sons, and she couldn't tell one from the other.

A muffled clamor could be heard through the windows, and the family looked out to see an entire police department on their feet, cheering and applauding for what we all want – a love that transcends and defeats the darkest hour.

The family gathered around Sarah's tape recorder that had captured the clamor and the love and the story. Jake and Cassie sat on one side of the table, and Sarah had an excuse to sit side-by-side with Josh.

"Why didn't you call us, Son?" Jake anxiously asked. Josh had no answer and couldn't look above Sarah's hands.

"Let's not talk about that, Jake. We're here now," Cassie enjoined.

Sarah commenced, "Josh was just starting to tell me what happened after he left Hi-Hi in Columbus."

"Oh, Dad! What a great guy he is. You've got to go see him," Josh urged.

"I will, Son. I will. Now, tell us your story."

Josh braced himself and began in carefully selected words. As his story unfolded in his memory, it became alive in every part of his body. The family listened in breathless anticipation, as Josh struggled to share his inexplicable pain.

Sarah's tape recorder could not see the pain that seized control of Josh's face, but it documented every nuance of every word that distorted his face. The tape recorder captured all the torment that Josh held inside, except for the horror of that day that Josh could not relive.

The family believed every word, and they heard Josh repeat over and over, "Ben was there," and "I asked Ben," and "Ben said."

"I couldn't have done it without Ben," Josh vowed. "I mean - except – except for - what happened – that day."

Josh's knees were twitching and bouncing, but his upper body was stilled by six caressing hands.

"Don't be afraid, Baby," Cassie soothed in her lullaby voice.

"Go on, Son, you know that you can tell us anything," Jake assured.

"No," Josh resisted and sealed his answer with a firm wag of his head. "I'm sorry, but I don't think I can ever tell you everything."

Sarah brought Josh's chin around and spoke to his heart through her eyes. "I think it might be easier tomorrow after you've gotten some rest."

The wag of Josh's head slowed but persisted. "I don't think so, Sarah. I can't tell – not even – not even to you, My Love."

Josh turned to Mom and Dad and swore on his brother's name. "Ben and I found that evil bastard - but – Ben had nothing – nothing to do with the rest - WITH WHAT I DID!"

Josh was rigid and unbending in his claim. He had related all that could be said without a confirming vote from Ben, and Ben had been absent for so long.

Jake tightened his grip on Josh's shoulder and responded with the stern conviction of love. "Ben has always had something to do with it, Josh because he has always been a part of you. Don't ever let go of that, Son."

"You go get some rest, Baby," Cassie murmured. She closed Josh's eyes, as she always could, with a stroke of his brow and running her fingers down his nose.

The family, Jake, Cassie, and yes, Sarah watched Josh being conducted to his cell. Although Sarah had watched many times, it never got easy, but she offered a bit of peace for Mom and Dad. "I think Josh is going to sleep better tonight."

Cassie encircled Sarah's neck and put her lips to Sarah's ear. "Thank you for being here for my Baby. I can't imagine what would have happened – what Josh would have done without..."

Cassie reluctantly let go as Sarah wriggled out of her arms. "You two go get some dinner."

"Will you come with us?" Jake invited.

"I would love to, Mr. and Mrs. Marshall." Sarah held up the tape recorder. "But I won't be able to sleep until I write this all down."

"I understand, Dear," Cassie endeared. "I just want you to know how much we love you already." Sarah received a kiss that only her own mother could surpass and a hug that only her own father could eclipse.

Sarah retreated to the sanctuary of her apartment, where she always hid under her downy comforter and daubed the tears and sniffles until her courage could catch up. The words from the tape recorder were excruciating to transcribe that night but somehow easier than those she had written before. Someone else had heard those words, someone who cared as much as she. She listened to every subtlety in Josh's words over and over, and she wrote...

Chapter 16

Session 6
9:35 am, September 23, 2001

Josh stuck his arm out the car window and gave one last wave to Mr. Nyugen before his figure in the rear-view mirror dwindled out of sight. The twelve-hour drive from Columbus to Plano was more than Josh could accept. Once his tires met the open road, he took advantage of the straight-a-ways and never let the speedometer fall below 90. He slowed only for the curves and then smoothed them out with the gas pedal smashed against the floorboard.

He scanned the prairie roads for the colors of black and white. He could not afford to blow past a highway patrol car that would impede his race to Plano. He didn't have time to waste on flashing red and blue lights.

It was Ben pushing Josh on. He didn't occupy a seat, but Josh heard him. "We've got to find her, Josh!"

And Josh talked to Ben, "Keep your eyes peeled, Ben, for a small white car with a blue door on the passenger side. I need your help, Ben."

Josh drove straight through while Ben kept pushing. "Don't stop, Josh. Hurry! 35 more miles, Josh. Take Exit 499A."

Plano was dark and asleep when Josh pulled into town. He found the first gas station/food mart and parked near the back. He couldn't remember when he had been so exhausted. He reclined the seat, rubbed his temples, and then pressed the butt of his hands against his eyes.

"We need sleep, Ben and food and a plan. I'm going to take a nap now, Ben."

"Ok, Josh."

"Josh?"

"Yeah, Ben."

"Are we really going to find Melinda?"

"You have my word, Ben. We'll find her. Now let me take a nap."

"Ok, Josh."

"Josh?"

Josh listened to Ben throughout the restless night. Ben's words were simple and true. "Do not fight darkness with darkness. Stay in the light."

Josh wanted to believe. He tried so hard in his dreams to believe. But his dreams were no match for the realities he had lived. This was not going to be easy. This was not going to be pretty. But Josh was ready. He could handle any battle that might ensue, so long as Ben would stay in the car.

Josh was startled awake by the violent wrapping on his car window. Fear gripped his mind and heart and rushed in faster than wide-eyed consciousness could quell. The policeman holstered his flashlight that had made those sharp bangs on the window.

Josh's fear of attack subsided and morphed into a dread of trouble. Now was not the time to make any trouble. Josh rolled down the window and spoke in raspy respect, "Good morning, Officer."

"Are you ok?" the officer inquired.

"Oh, yes sir," Josh assured.

The officer informed, "The owner of this gas station called us because he thought you might be dead. You sure looked dead."

"I just needed a little sleep, Sir."

"Well this is not an overnight parking area, but it's better than falling asleep on the road. May I see your driver's license and registration?"

Josh handed over his license and prayed for the best.

"So, you're from Kansas," the officer noted.

"Yes, Sir."

"Are you coming or going, Mr. Marshall?"

"I'm heading home Sir, as soon as I get some gas and food."

"Make sure you get a big cup of coffee as well, Mr. Marshall, and drive safely."

Josh's shoulders dropped in relief, and he breathed big sighs of alleviation, as he watched the officer drive away. "That was close, Ben. We've got to be more careful. Let's get some gas now."

Josh was just as methodical as he and Ben had been with the semi-truck. He checked the oil, water, and the air pressure in the tires. He washed the windshield but couldn't get it as clean as Ben would have.

Josh was too anxious about his mission to be hungry, but he needed that big cup of coffee. Passing by the pastry aisle, he spotted Twinkies and Ding Dongs. He couldn't resist grabbing one of each. They were Ben's favorites.

"Do you have a city map, Sir?" Josh asked the store clerk.

There was only one map left in the rack, and the clerk packed it in the bag with Ben's favorites.

Josh unfolded the map in the car. He spread it wide so Ben could see. "How about we start cruising the north/south streets first, Ben?"

Josh didn't hear Ben's response, but he knew that Ben would agree. Josh figured that in a couple of days and with two or three tanks of gas, he could take Ben down every street in Plano.

Few would believe that Ben was really there, keeping his eyes peeled and talking incessantly to Josh. But to Josh, Ben's presence was as real as his memory, and his voice resonated in Josh's head. Two brothers were in the car, and nothing would ever change that.

It was early in the morning, and there were still lots of cars parked in driveways and on the side of the streets. Every time Ben spotted a small white car parked along the curb, Josh would stop and walk casually down the sidewalk to take a quick, nonchalant look at the passenger-side door.

Often, he would have to divert from his planned path to follow a small white car for blocks until Ben could get a glimpse of the right side of the car.

Half-way through the day, Josh's confidence was waning. Dozens of small white cars had caught Ben's eye, and dozens had dashed Josh's hopes. He remembered having admonished Ben, "There's only a small chance that we can find her, Ben." And now, there was no one helping them to look.

But Ben would not give in. He would not let his dream die, and he kept spurring Josh on. "We can't quit now, Josh. Just a little longer, PLEASE!"

"Ok, Ben. We'll keep looking until the cows come home."

By the end of the day, Josh's mind and body were depleted. He hadn't eaten or truly rested for so long.

Ben knew his brother's limitations and cajoled, "Don't worry, Josh. Don't give up. We'll find Melinda tomorrow. I know we will. And Josh?"

"Yeah, Ben."

"You can have my Twinkie and Ding Dong. I'm not very hungry."

"Thanks, Ben, but..."

"Go ahead, Josh, and then take a good long nap. I'll wake you when the sun comes up tomorrow, and we'll drive down all the east/west streets."

Josh pulled to the curb in a quiet neighborhood of modest homes. Kitchen lights and porch lights were just being turned on, and Josh turned off the headlights before his wheels came to rest. He peered at the gauges by the dim street light glow and then turned off the engine.

"We need to get gas again first thing in the morning, Ben."

"Don't forget to check the oil and water, Josh."

"You won't let me forget, Ben."

Josh reclined the seat and slid into the lowest possible profile. He pulled the brim of his cap over his eyes to dampen the glow of the street light. He zipped his jacket all the way to his chin and slipped on his warm winter gloves. He was too tired to eat, and besides, maybe Ben would want his favorites in the morning.

It was an uneasy sleep, more fitful and broken than usual. Josh was agitated by foreboding thoughts of the evil he was seeking. He struggled to bury revenge deep in his gut and battled to remember Ben's words, "Stay on the side of the light." His gut churned from fear and growled from lack of food. His mind flashed with vivid images of that young girl whose frightened face begged for help. And Ben's voice echoed through the night, "Melinda Miles!"

Hours dragged painfully by until the street lights began to flicker off, as the sun pushed its way slightly above the horizon. Any sound would jar Josh awake, particularly the sound of a muffler scraping over the hump of a driveway entrance.

Josh sank lower in his seat and listened to a car door squeak open and bang shut. The front door of the house was slammed even louder.

Josh peeked over the dashboard, with only a sliver of gap between the brim of his cap and the concealment of the dash. Fifty feet away and on the other side of the street, a small white car reflected the dimming luminescence of the streetlight.

"I'll bet that's it, Josh!" Ben blurted from inside Josh's mind. Josh hoped and feared at the same time that Ben was right.

"Calm down, Ben. We don't know that's it. I have to go check it out. If I find a blue door on the other side, I'm going to run back and call the police. Now remember, Ben, stay in the car."

"I'll be right behind you, Josh."

"Yeah, Ben, I know you will."

Josh stepped out of the car and left the door unlatched and silent. He pushed on the door just enough to make the dome light go out. He plunged his gloved hands in his jacket pockets like a guy on an early morning walk and crossed the street. He kept his head down and maintained his casual stride. He slowed as he passed the rear of the white car and turned his head ever-so-slightly.

At the sight of a faded blue door, Josh's muscles locked, and his body froze in place. That was his mistake.

Chapter 17

Those were the last words Josh spoke into the tape recorder or to anyone about that fateful day that condemned him to incarceration and destined him to find a love that could never be consummated. He revelled in old memories with Mom and Dad but spoke nothing about the future. He treasured every moment with Sarah and gathered new memories, as the days slipped by.

No amount of prodding or pleading could dislodge the truth that only Josh and Ben knew. Josh's day of reckoning was nigh, but he could not divulge the secret that taunted him. All he knew how to do was to bear the shame, accept the punishment, and lay his heart on the floor.

Three days before the trial, Phillip McCay made one last appeal to Josh. "Doggonit, Josh." Phil sat hunched in the chair with his elbows on his knees and his head in his hands. "It's just a crying shame that we're going to lose this case."

Phil lifted his head, straightened his arms, and rested his hands on his knees. "I know that I could convince a jury to decide in your favor, but I need to know what really happened that day."

Josh twitched and swished from side to side in impossible torment. He wanted to say what everyone needed to hear, but he couldn't form the words. They were stuck in his throat like peanut butter without milk. He couldn't accept his actions that defiled everything that was Ben. It was like trying to let go of believing in Santa Claus. It was like trying to let go of the last shred of Ben's decency.

Phil knelt in front of Josh and tried one more futile time. "I know that you had no choice but to kill that beast, Josh. But the jury won't know that unless you tell them." Phil waited, hoping, yet knowing that his efforts were in vain.

For three more days, no power on earth could unlock the untold horror that Josh was prepared to carry to his grave.

Jake and Cassie didn't fare any better in persuading their son to save himself. The sweet enticements of Cassie's motherly affection only made Josh cry more.

In desperation, Jake tried the one thing he hated most. "You'd better tell the rest of your story, Josh. Don't make me beat it out of you!"

Josh yielded to his Daddy's feigned wrath. "I'm sorry, Daddy. I deserve any whuppin' you need to give me. I just can't."

Even Sarah's petitions were of no avail, no matter how soft or harsh. "I need you, Josh. Please fight for us."

Josh answered with the love that tore at his heart. "I need you too, Sarah, but I can't have you. There is no fight left in me. I am nothing without Ben."

"YES, YOU ARE!" Sarah bawled in defiance. "YOU MAKE ME SO MAD! You are the love of my life, and you're going to throw that away!"

Josh sat with his hands cupped in his lap. He remembered his words to Ben. "All I knew is that I wanted to be with you more than her."

Josh now had someone he wanted to kiss more than a couple of times. But Ben had not spoken to Josh for so very long. And, without Ben's forgiveness and without Ben's blessing, life and love could not go on.

Josh could not excuse it, and he could not explain it. All he could say was, "I'm sorry, Sarah."

The trial was set for 9:00 am on a Wednesday. Josh and Ben were born on a Wednesday. Ben was killed on a Wednesday. Josh had met Sarah on a Wednesday. Josh figured that Wednesday was as good of a day as any to live or die.

Sarah woke Josh at 6:00 am with a breakfast that he would not eat. All Josh was thinking about was a Twinkie and a Ding Dong.

Sarah dropped to her knees and begged, "Josh, PLEASE! I can't bear it. You know how much I love you. Please don't leave me. Fight for me. Fight for us. Tell me the rest of your story."

Josh did not dare approach the love of his life. He had nothing to offer her except more pain. He knew what he was giving up. He was giving up freedom and family. He was passing up a love that could have lasted forever. But he hadn't heard from Ben in a very long time, and he didn't know what else to do.

Josh remained on his bunk and expressed his deepest regrets. "I love you too, Sarah. But what you're asking, I cannot do. I WISH TO GOD I COULD!"

The police escort came and helped Sarah to her feet. They couldn't ease her heartbreak. They could only fight back their own tears. They and so many others in the police department had been hoping for a happy ending for a love story that had held them all in its grips.

The officers reluctantly performed their duty-bound procedure and placed the cuffs on Josh's surrendering wrists. They walked behind him, allowing Sarah to cling to his arm.

Josh kept his eyes fixed forward as he was herded into the courtroom. The corner of his eye detected Mom and Dad in the front row of the gallery. Mom was on the aisle side, holding back her tears and giving all the solace her eyes could offer. Dad was on her left with his jaw clenched tight in all the courage he could convey. On Dad's left, emerged a figure of grace and understanding that transcended Josh's mortal world. Gretchen's uniform was adorned with brass and ribbons and her beloved cross of Jesus. Her very presence commanded Josh's jaw to drop and his heart to rise in his throat. Gretchen blessed Josh with a hand on his cheek and reminded, "Tell them what you were fighting for."

Josh plodded forward with his mind full of questions. "What do you think, Ben? What should I say? I need you, Ben." But Josh had not heard Ben's voice since that day that he saw the faded blue door on the right side of the small white car.

Phillip McCay sat next to Josh and laid his pad and pen on the table in trepidation. This was not looking like his finest hour, but he would give Josh every ounce of fight in his defense. Sarah sat on Josh's left and kept a steady hold on his arm.

The prosecution laid out all their statements and photographs and sat at ease, ready for the impending slaughter. They knew of the heartache and affliction the defendant had suffered, but that only led them to the conclusion of motive and premeditation. They knew that the defendant was the last person to see the victim alive, and that was their proof of opportunity.

The Honorable Judge Clemens entered. "All rise," the bailiff directed. Even Josh rose of his own volition, ready to face his consequences. "Ben, I need you, Ben."

The bailiff announced the case. There was no charge of manslaughter or negligent homicide. The prosecution had blindly and boldly entered only one charge, first-degree murder.

Judge Clemens gave the jury its instructions. Then Clemens called for the defendant's plea. McCay rose to speak for his client who couldn't find the words. "My client pleads absolute, unequivocal innocence, Your Honor."

Clemens called for the opening statements, and the prosecution took the floor. McKay knew what would be included in that statement, but he took copious notes of every damning syllable that left the mouth of Assistant District Attorney David Barstow.

"Ladies and Gentlemen of the jury, this is not an easy task for me. I take no pleasure in presenting the facts in this case. They are cold, hard facts. They will not be easy to hear, but they are facts all the same."

"When you hear the defendant's story, you will be touched by the agony and suffering that drove him to murder. You will be tempted to forgive because you feel his pain. He lost a beloved brother in a violent confrontation, and I cannot imagine the anguish and misery that has caused him."

"He was blessed with a family that tried to console and help him to heal. But Josh Marshall could not let go of the hate and malice he carried in his gut."

"The People will show that Mr. Marshall sought out his brother's killer. After months of a carefully planned and exhaustive search, he found the man that was responsible for his brother's death. It wasn't a moment of insanity or a fit of momentary rage that caused the defendant to snap his victim's neck. It was vengeance. It was a deliberate, premeditated murder."

"Again, you may be inclined to forgive the defendant for his actions. You may even think that you might have done the same if you were in his place. But that does not change the fact of law that no one can take a life in exchange or retaliation for another life."

"The defendant will receive a fair trial, and the facts will speak for themselves. But, remember, the defendant's victim also had a right to a fair trial. The defendant chose to be his victim's judge, jury, and executioner."

"The defense has entered a plea of innocence. Yet, the defendant has not come forth with a statement as to how and why he is innocent. That is because he knows the gravity of his decision. He knows the gruesome nature of his actions, and he cannot accept them himself. Nor can you accept them, ladies and gentlemen."

"Murder is murder, regardless of the reason. There is no excuse for murder."

Barstow pointed directly at Josh and flatly accused, "That young man murdered another human being, and that cannot be excused or forgiven."

Barstow took his seat, satisfied with his elocution and certain of the velocity of his first pitch from the mound.

Barstow's comments had no visible effect on Josh. He was barely paying attention. He was listening for Ben. But there was a reason that his father, Jake, was flanked on one side by Cassie and on the other by Gretchen. It required both of them to hold the seething fatherhood in his seat. David Barstow would not have finished his opening remarks without Cassie and

Gretchen wrapping their legs around Jake's ankles and locking their arms around his shoulders.

Josh was mumbling the stirrings in his head. "I told Ben I was going to call the police - but – I screwed up, Ben." Only Sarah and McCay could decipher Josh's ramblings, and Sarah silenced them with her fingers over his lips.

McCay approached the jury to give his opening remarks. His demeanor was much less intimidating and much more inviting. He knew a little about each of the jurors from the jury selection process. Some of them had an unshakable allegiance to the letter of the law. Others had questions about where the law ends, and humanity begins. And, there were a few who responded to feelings more than reason. McCay had to find a way to speak to them all. He looked at twelve pairs of eyes and began.

"There are many kinds of facts, Ladies and Gentlemen of Texas. There is the fact that the sun rises and sets every day. There is the fact that good and evil are at constant war in this world."

"Josh Marshall watched the sun rise and set with his brother every day for twenty-three years. And, it is a fact that he loved his brother more than life. His brother, Ben was everything Josh knew of good, and it is a fact that Ben died at the hands of evil."

"It is not a fact that Josh wanted that evil dead. He wanted to defeat that evil and bring some meaning to his brother's death by rescuing another soul from evil's grip. The prosecution failed to mention or perhaps failed to recognize that Josh was on a mission. His quest was to grant Ben's final wish that a young girl, named Melinda Miles, was returned safely home."

"We are now certain that Melinda was abducted by the man we choose to call the murder victim. Ben Marshall died trying to rescue her, and that is what Josh could not let go of. He made a sacred oath to his brother to continue the search. He swore that he would not rest until his brother's final wish was granted."

"Melinda Miles is now safe with her family because Josh, with the spiritual help of Ben, took her home. A man died in the process, but he is not the victim. Melinda was the victim. Ben was a victim. Josh is still a victim. But, in a greater sense, Josh and Ben are the victors and the heroes."

"The prosecution also stated that Josh had not provided a statement in defense of his actions. That is because Josh chose not to defend his actions. He chooses still to own his actions and their possible consequences, as belonging only to himself. Doing so may cost him his life, but there's something you need to understand about Josh, ladies, and gentlemen. In

Josh's mind and heart, he is risking only half a life. The other half already rests in peace."

McCay crossed the courtroom and picked up one of Sarah's two-dozen copies of her manuscript of Josh and Ben's story. "Your Honor, I have here, and I would like to submit into evidence the statement of Josh Marshall. It is the truest account of the events leading up to the death of our nameless "victim," whom I shall heretofore refer to as the assailant."

"OBJECTION, your Honor," Barstow roared. "The People have not been provided this statement or any other information from the defense."

The Honorable John Clemens accepted the manuscript from McCay and began leafing through the pages. "Mr. Barstow, I understand that you have had the defendant incarcerated for over thirty days and that you have not been able to procure one word from him regarding his guilt or innocence. I will not deny him this opportunity to make a statement. Objection overruled."

The Honorable Clemens then addressed McCay. "There are over forty pages of statement here, Counselor."

"Yes, your Honor," McCay acknowledged. "Perhaps forty minutes of the jury's time to understand what would otherwise take days of testimony."

Clemens peered over his glasses to ensure that Barstow had no further objection. "This court will be in recess until..."

The bailiff scanned the daily court schedule and held up two fingers. "Until 2:00 pm this afternoon, allowing the jury time to review the defendant's statement."

The bailiff passed out the copies and jurors immediately and irresistibly began engrossing themselves in Sarah's gripping narrative. As they were led from the courtroom, they stumbled and bumped into each other, unwilling to divert their eyes from the next sentence.

Barstow accepted his copy with a grumble. McCay had done it again. Barstow was ready to call his first witness, but McCay had upstaged him and had stolen the jury's attention.

Chapter 18

McCay met privately with the family, and they huddled to hear his game plan. "I am certain that the prosecution is going to point out that we have provided nothing more than a heart-warming story of two devoted brothers and a young girl that needed to go home."

Phil spoke to Josh in soft, but stern words. "I have character witnesses, but I have no witness of what happened on the only day that matters now. The prosecution has eyewitnesses and expert witnesses."

Phil could tell that Josh was listening, though he sat with his eyes cast down. Now and again, his lips quivered in an impossible desire to speak.

"Josh, it's game time," Phil emphatically insisted, "and my star players are on the disabled list. Ben or Melinda Miles can't carry the ball for you, but I'm sure Ben is sitting on the sidelines, cheering you on."

Josh's face contorted and deformed in an agony that was fearful to watch. It was as if the knife in his heart had just been twisted. "BEN HASN'T TALKED TO ME SINCE I KILLED THAT MAN!"

Josh looked at Jake and Cassie and begged forgiveness. "I've really lost my brother now. I don't think he will ever talk to me again."

He looked at Gretchen, who understood the deepest sorrow and understood unfailing forgiveness. "I don't think Ben can forgive me for walking on the dark side."

Gretchen walked around behind Josh and laid her hands on his head. "Ben is still with you, Little Brother. He would never desert you. That, you have to believe."

Gretchen put her cheek against Josh's and pressed her hand over his heart. "Keep your heart open, and you will hear him again."

"OH, GRETCHEN! I want to believe that, but HOW?" Josh lamented in an anguish that would have ripped apart the most stalwart of hearts.

Gretchen wrapped Josh's neck in her arms and spoke a phrase that only Josh could hear. "What was the last thing you heard Ben say?"

Josh thought about everything that Ben had ever said. He tried to sort out what was real and what was only imagined. But everything about Ben was real and honest and pure.

"The very last thing, Josh," Gretchen whispered. "What was it?"

Josh clasped his big sister's hand and uttered those final words. "I'll be right behind you, Josh."

Josh's head fell to the table, and the "thump" echoed off the walls. Josh cried like a young boy who was so lost, and so alone. He was not alone. He had family all around him, reaching to touch his pain. But Josh couldn't feel anything but hopeless despair.

Gretchen laid the full weight of her love on her brother's back. "And that is where Ben is, Josh. He's right behind you. You never deserted him, and he will never desert you."

Gretchen could not stop Josh's tears, but she could always lull him to sleep, gliding her finger down his forehead, between his eyes, and down his nose. So, Josh slept but still twitched at every memory of Ben's words. "Keep going, Josh. We've got to find her, Josh. You can have my Twinkie, Josh. I'll wake you when the sun comes up, Josh. I'll be right behind you, Josh. Josh?"

It was Sarah who woke Josh with a nibble on his ear. "We have to go back into court, Josh. You and me, Sweetheart. You and me."

Josh shot straight up, not sure of where he was. Ben wasn't there, but Sarah was. He stood, although he had no idea of where he had to go. He could only follow the voice that commanded him and the vision that consumed him. That's all he needed to know.

Sarah walked backward, directly in front of Josh, and Josh looked at nothing but those affectionate eyes. It didn't matter where he was or where he was going, as long as he stayed with those eyes.

Josh sat at the defendant's table because Sarah sat. He breathed because Sarah breathed.

Jake and Cassie did not recognize the shell of their son. They had never known him to fall and not get up.

Gretchen prayed because she knew that there was only one hope for Josh. The Father in Heaven needed to speak to him, and Josh would hear the Word of God only through the voice of Ben.

The Honorable Judge Clemens called the court back into session and directed the prosecution to call its first witness.

"Your Honor, if the court will allow," Barstow requested, "I would like to present an observation regarding the defendant's statement."

"Proceed, Mr. Prosecutor."

"This manuscript is nothing more than an embellished biography of a man's happy life with his brother and the pain he suffered at the loss of his brother," Barstow rejected. "It contains nothing pertinent to the homicide in question. It does, however, provide ample motive for the charge of premeditated murder."

Clemens leveled an authoritative look of warning and advised, "Mr. Barstow, you are perilously close to trying to instruct this court in the law. And I will not have you instructing the jury as to the conclusions they should draw from the defendant's statement."

Clemens turned to address the jury. "You will disregard the prosecution's opinion regarding the document you have just read." He turned back to Barstow and cautioned, "You will present your evidence and testimony through the proper examination of witnesses. That is my instruction in the law."

"Yes, Your Honor," Barstow submitted. "My apologies to the court."

Barstow had strike one against him, but he was not done swinging. "I would like to call to the stand Detective Jeremy Hornsby."

Hornsby took the stand with no qualms or misgivings. He was there to answer questions, to provide testimony, and to do his duty. He did not consider himself to be a witness for the prosecution or for the defense. He was there as a witness to the truth as he knew it.

"Detective Hornsby," Barstow began, "you are an investigator with the Columbus, Georgia Police Department. Is that correct?"

"Yes, Sir, for fourteen years."

"Fourteen years," Barstow reiterated. "I would think that in that amount of time, you would have been promoted beyond your current duties."

Hornsby was very comfortable in responding, "I have been offered a couple of promotions, Sir, but I have turned them down."

"And why would you do that, Detective?" Barstow prodded.

"I am a firm believer in the "Peter Principle," Hornsby advocated.

"Ah!" Barstow boasted of his breadth of knowledge. "I am aware of that philosophic principle. Would you please expound on it for the court?"

Hornsby gratuitously obliged. "The Peter Principle simply states that in any organization, one rises to their level of incompetence."

"Please go on, Detective."

Hornsby's response became a bit more begrudging. "Most promotions are given, based on how well you have done your current job, not on how qualified you are for the next promotion. If that practice continues, you will likely promote to a position for which you are not qualified. I choose to stay where I am because I am very good at what I do."

"That is most commendable, Detective," Barstow patronized. "Now, I understand that you investigated the events surrounding the death of the defendant's brother, Ben Marshall."

"Yes, Sir, for many months."

"And I presume you used every reasonable resource at your disposal in that investigation," Barstow continued to steer the testimony.

"Yes, Sir, and I wish we had more resources to…"

"And in your many years of investigative experience," Barstow barged in, "how would you contrast the defendant's actions with others who have lost loved ones to violent crimes? Would you say he was overly zealous to find his brother's killer?"

"EXCUSE ME!" McCay thundered. It wasn't proper court protocol, but his point came across even to Barstow.

"Let me rephrase the question, Detective. Isn't it true that the defendant hounded your office almost daily regarding your progress on the investigation?"

Hornsby, who regarded the rights of the victim over the rights of the perpetrator, deftly responded, "No more than my wife hounds me to fix that leaky faucet."

Barstow blustered over the chittering in the courtroom. "But the defendant did call incessantly, unable to wait for the due process of law to bring his brother's killer to justice! Did he not?"

"He did that, Sir."

Barstow ended his questions before another contradictory word could be uttered. "I have no further questions of this witness, Your Honor."

"Does the defense wish to cross-examine?" Clemens followed.

"Absolutely, Your Honor," McCay asserted.

McCay cast an adversarial glare at Barstow on his way by. Barstow paid no attention, but if he had, he would have seen that glare that says in no uncertain terms, "Just wait until I get your ass outside."

McCay then approached the witness as a respected fellow officer of the court. "Detective Hornsby, I cannot imagine the sleepless nights you must have had during an investigation of such magnitude and gravity."

Hornsby shuffled his feet and wrung his hands. "Yes, Sir."

McCay nodded his head in empathy. "And when the defendant called you to inquire about your investigation, how did he ask?"

"How's that, Sir?" Hornsby didn't understand.

"Did he ask you about your progress in finding the killer of his brother?"

Hornsby thought long and hard about the most important question he had been asked so far. "No, Sir, not once."

"What did he ask you, Detective?"

Hornsby looked at Josh to confirm that his memory was correct. "He always asked if we had any leads in finding Melinda Miles."

McCay waited until Hornsby's eyes came back to his, and Hornsby went on, "I never had anything to give him." Hornsby struggled to maintain the rigid composure required for his job, but he just couldn't do it. "Yes, I had sleepless nights."

Hornsby's emotions surfaced, and he could not hold them back. "Countless suppers went cold while I poured through statements and photographs. I missed my kids' birthdays and soccer games, while I searched for a needle in a haystack."

McCay conveyed his understanding. "If only you had more help, Detective. If only you had more resources to..."

"NO!" Hornsby refuted. "A dozen more officers would not have found Melinda Miles." Hornsby looked back to Josh in amazement. "I don't know how that young man did it. He had to have sifted through every wisp of hay in the stack and spent every waking hour."

"And if Josh Marshall had not done that?" McCay advanced.

Hornsby faced McCay with a conviction that went beyond professional expertise and beyond common perception. "Then, Melinda Miles would not be safely home today."

McCay had nothing more to add. Nothing further could have increased the impact of Hornsby's testimony. "Thank you, Detective. No further questions, Your Honor."

Detective Hornsby was dismissed, and McCay took his victory stride across the room. McKay gave a wink to the family, who were crying the first happy tears McKay had been able to inspire. They were tears of pride and hope and courage.

Chapter 19

Barstow winced at the second strike that had been dealt, but he was undeterred. It was still only the first inning, and he called his next batter. "I would like to call to the witness stand Detective Todd Mitchell."

Mitchell took the stand and made the mistake of glaring at Josh. Josh returned the mutual dislike and distrust with an ominous look that made Mitchell squirm in the chair. This was the man who had disrespected Sarah, and Josh would have given anything to have his hand around that throat again.

"Detective Mitchell," Barstow addressed, "you were the first to question the defendant, were you not?"

"Yes, I was," Mitchell succinctly answered.

"And what was the suspect's demeanor? Was he cooperative?" Barstow prompted.

"Not at all," Mitchell protested. "He wouldn't even give us his name. He just called himself his brother's keeper."

"And didn't he become violent during your questioning?" Barstow asked, with a turn of his head to the jury.

Mitchell noticeably fidgeted and rubbed his chin. "I asked him his brother's name and – and - he went wild. He – uh – smashed the table against the wall and then – uh – attacked me."

"Attacked, indeed, Detective!" Barstow amplified. "Isn't it true that the defendant threw you bodily through the air and against that same wall?"

Cassie was aghast at her son's actions, but Jake had to stifle a snicker. They knew their boy's strength, and they were learning more about his will. Sarah had written that story and gave a confirming and congratulatory nod to Mom and Dad.

"Well," Mitchell minimalized, "I wouldn't say through the air."

"And wasn't the assistance of three officers required to subdue the prisoner?" Barstow emphasized.

The emasculated detective argued, "That was a trained response by those officers. I did not require assistance."

"No further questions, Your Honor."

Barstow took his seat with a self-satisfied air as if he had gotten a base hit. Mitchell surveyed the courtroom, avoiding any eye contact.

McCay rose to stand behind Josh and called out his challenge. "Detective Mitchell?" Mitchell did not respond. He was looking for the most expeditious exit.

"DETECTIVE MITCHELL!" McCay repeated in a tone of authority that demanded Mitchell's attention. Mitchell turned his head toward McCay but refused to look Josh in the eye.

"I noticed you exchanging glares with my client when you took the stand," McCay observed, "and I thought I noticed you squirm a bit in your chair. Does my client make you uncomfortable or nervous?"

"Of course not! I've handled tougher criminals," Mitchell defended.

McCay charged the witness stand as if he might vault over the railing. "Your Honor," McCay submitted, "would you please instruct the witness to not refer to my client as a criminal."

"Detective Mitchell," Clemens corrected, "you know that the defendant is not a criminal unless he is convicted of a crime."

Mitchell was now visibly shaken, and McCay seized the opportunity. "Being thrown against a wall must have not only been somewhat painful, but it must also have been very embarrassing."

It was obvious that Mitchell wished he had a place to hide. He lowered his head and ran his hand through his hair.

"Did you meet with Josh Marshall on a second occasion?" McCay pushed.

"Yes, the next day," Mitchell admitted.

"And did Josh display any violence that day?" McCay already knew the answer, and it was an answer he would not allow Mitchell to avoid.

"He was very mouthy – and – threatening," Mitchell accused.

"Very threatening, I understand," McCay cited. "Is it true that he threatened to rip your head off?"

"Well, yeah, but..." Mitchell tried to deflect.

"Now why do you suppose he would do that?" McCay wrangled.

"I told you, the guy is nuts!" Mitchell barked.

McCay took three steps to retrieve a folder. "Were Officers - uh..." McCay held his glasses to his eyes as if he was reading from the folder. "were Officers Hendrix and Levine in the room with you?"

"Yes, they were, and they can verify..." Mitchell contended.

"Could Josh's provocation for his threat," McCay interrupted, "have been that you called Ms. Sarah Langston, who was present in the room..." McCay pretended to read from the folder again, "an uppity little bitch?"

Mitchell did not need to answer, his down-cast eyes were sufficient. He was done for, and he knew it.

"Where I come from, Detective," McCay avowed, "if you speak in that manner to a lady in my presence, them's fight'n words."

Clemens quelled the murmur that was beginning amongst the jury with a light tap of his gavel.

McCay shook the folder in Mitchell's face. "And there was other violence in the room that day, wasn't there?"

Mitchell's response was reduced to a nod, as McCay handed the folder to Clemens. Judge Clemens opened the folder and discovered two blank sheets of paper. There were no statements and no words of testimony in that folder. McCay never said there were. It was a ruse and a gamble, but Mitchell was condemning himself just fine.

"Is it correct that Josh's hands were cuffed, his ankles were shackled, and your hand was on his throat when he threatened to rip your head off?" McCay goaded further.

Mitchell tried to make himself as small as possible in the chair.

"And wasn't Josh still in cuffs and shackles when you punched him in the gut and struck his jaw?" McCay charged.

Mitchell could not think of a saving response. All he could do was tremble under the weight of his deeds.

"I'm sorry, Detective, I didn't hear your answer," McCay pressed.

Mitchell drew in a deep breath and let it out in defeat. "YES!"

McCay turned his back on the disgrace that happened to wear a badge. "No further questions, Your Honor."

"The witness may step down," Clemens directed, "if his spine can handle it."

Mitchell had no choice but to begin his walk of shame. His badge was no longer a shield against the stares and scowls he could feel as he counted his steps to the big double exit doors that were his only escape.

The prosecutor, Barstow, bowed his head and heaved a sigh, knowing he had been tagged out, trying to steal second base.

"Your next witness, Mr. Prosecutor?" Clemens spurred.

Barstow had planned to call his next detective, Hallstrom, but with Mitchell's fly-out to center field, it was time to change the batting order. He leafed through his papers and pulled out the list of names of his three eyewitnesses.

"Your Honor, I call Mrs. Dorothy O'Connor to the stand." Mrs. O'Connor placed her hand on the bible she lived by. She gave the judge a sweet nod of her truest of intentions.

Barstow asked similar questions of each of the three eyewitnesses, and each of their answers were obviously different. "Mrs. O'Connor, do you see in this courtroom the man whom you saw fleeing the crime scene?"

Mrs. O'Connor canvassed the room and answered, "No, I don't see him."

Barstow showed the photograph of Josh with his wiry hair and scruffy beard. "Mrs. O'Connor, is this the man you picked out of the line-up?"

"Yes, that's him," Mrs. O'Connor was sure.

Barstow walked over to Josh and pointed. "This is the man you picked out."

Mrs. O'Connor's eyes widened, and her fingers masked her lips. "Oh no, that can't be. That's such a nice-looking young man."

The beleaguered Barstow almost pleaded with Mrs. O'Connor, "When you saw this man running across the lawn, did you see him carrying anything on his shoulder?"

"Yes, I did," Mrs. O'Connor was adamant. "It looked like a rolled-up blanket or rug, but who would steal a rug?"

Barstow chose to cut his losses with this witness. "Your Honor, may the court record show that Mrs. O'Connor identified the man in the photograph, who does happen to be the defendant."

Judge Clemens let the prosecution off the hook with a patronizing nod. "Continue, Mr. Barstow."

"I have no further questions of this witness," Barstow gave in.

McCay took his turn with each witness and engaged them in a more congenial conversation. "How far away was the fleeing man when you saw him, Mrs. O'Connor?"

"Oh, I was on my front porch. I live four houses down the street. I certainly wasn't going to get any closer," Mrs. O'Connor declared.

"That was very wise, Mrs. O'Connor," McCay commended, "but I'm sure that you keep a watchful eye on your neighborhood."

"You better bet I do," Mrs. O'Connor boasted. "I like to think that I'm a good neighbor."

"Yes, Mrs. O'Connor, we all need good neighbors like you."

McCay turned to face the jury as he continued to address Mrs. O'Connor. "The lots in your neighborhood are fifty-feet-wide. So, you saw this man running from the crime scene from two hundred feet away. Does that sound right, Mrs. O'Connor?"

"If you say so," Mrs. O'Connor conceded.

McCay paused to catch a glimpse of question in each juror's eyes. Then, he turned back to recognize the ally he had made. "Thank you, Mrs. O'Connor. Your testimony has been most valuable."

Judge Clemens excused the witness and McCay escorted Mrs. O'Connor from the witness stand and paraded her back to her seat. He could hear the collective expiration of relief from Josh's family, and he delivered a self-congratulatory scowl at Barstow.

Chapter 20

That was the third out for Barstow, and he was now on the defensive. All he could do was hope that McKay's team didn't score the first run. He hesitantly called his next eyewitness. He approached Mr. Frederickson with Josh's photo in hand, but he did not ask him to identify the suspect in the courtroom.

"Mr. Frederickson, how many gunshots did you hear, before you saw the defendant running from the crime scene?"

"I thought it was three," Frederickson answered. Barstow gave a dejected look of frustration.

"Well, I guess one of them could have been an echo," Frederickson relented.

This was a contradiction of the police report of two gunshots, and Barstow decided to pitch an intentional walk. He relinquished his witness to the cross-examination of the defense.

"Mr. Frederickson," McCay respectfully enjoined, "are you an early riser?"

"Yes, Sir," Frederickson was proud to say. "I'm out there at the crack of dawn every day getting my newspaper. That's when I seen the fella."

"So, it wasn't very light out when you saw the man fleeing," McCay pointed out.

"No, Sir, but I seen his scraggly hair, and I seen his car," Frederickson countered.

"Can you describe the car for me, Mr. Frederickson?"

"Sure – uh- it was one of them foreign jobs they make in Japan or Germany or somewhere."

McCay looked around again for the questioning eyes in the courtroom and offered, "Thank you, Mr. Frederickson. You have been very helpful."

McCay walked back to his seat and then turned about. "One more question, Mr. Frederickson. Does the defendant look like the man you saw fleeing the crime scene?"

Mr. Frederickson studied Josh's unimposing figure and stoic face. "Well – uh, he has a clean shave now, and – uh, he could have had a haircut – but..."

For no apparent reason, Josh looked directly at Mr. Frederickson. Perhaps it was because he heard the voice of a man whose word he could trust.

There was something in Josh's humble and non-hostile gaze that made Mr. Frederickson respond, "That looks like a guy I'd like to have a beer with. I don't think he could be the guy I seen."

"Thank you again, Mr. Frederickson. No further questions, Your Honor." McCay unceremoniously took his seat and watched Barstow, who really didn't want to come out of the dugout again. McKay had hit a home run that drove in his intentional walk and had two runs on the scoreboard. But Barstow willed himself to call one more eyewitness.

"Mrs. Williams, how many gunshots did you hear?" Barstow questioned.

"I'm not quite sure," Mrs. Williams apologized. "After the first gunshot, we all laid on the floor and covered our ears."

Barstow nodded in defeat on that point and struggled to think of another question.

Mrs. Williams volunteered her theory. "I'll bet that was a body wrapped in a blanket over that guy's shoulder."

"Ah," Barstow jumped at the chance, "did it look like a body wrapped in a blanket?"

"How am I supposed to know what a body wrapped in a blanket over a man's shoulder looks like?" Mrs. Williams disavowed.

Barstow retreated back to the dugout, knowing that he had allowed another runner on base. "No further questions, Your Honor."

"Mrs. Williams," McCay greeted, "where do you live, relative to the crime scene?"

"Right next door," Mrs. Williams answered in dismay. "That's why I was so scared."

"Certainly, you would be, Mrs. Williams," McCay empathized. "and of all the witnesses we have heard from, you must have had the best view of the man running to his car."

"I would think so," Mrs. Williams agreed. "I heard that first gunshot, and as soon as I got off the floor, I peeked through the Venetian blinds."

"That must have been so frightening, Mrs. Williams," McCay appreciated. "Would you please look at the defendant and tell me; does he frighten you?"

Once again, Josh was drawn to looking at the witness, whose voice sounded more like his Grandma than his Momma. His puppy dog eyes drooped in remembrance of warm cookies and milk.

"No," Mrs. Williams answered. "I would – I'd like to give him a hug."

"I thank you for sharing, Mrs. Williams," McCay praised, "and the Great State of Texas thanks you. No further questions Your Honor."

That was McCay's equivalent of hitting that fastball right back at the pitcher's head.

Barstow was still ducking that ball speeding toward his head when he called Detective Hallstrom to the stand. He had to get this inning over with and get back in the batter's box. His starting pitcher was done, and his bullpen was nearly depleted. But Hallstrom was his star reliever.

"Detective, I don't think we need your testimony regarding the defendant's presence at the crime scene. He has confessed that he was there in a sworn statement."

"Objection, Your Honor," McCay railed against the claim. "My client stated only that he found a small white car with a blue passenger-side door, in a quiet neighborhood."

In a failure to salvage what was left of his shattered composure, Barstow ranted at McCay, "Ah, Come on! How many white cars with a blue door do you think there are in Plano?"

"Mr. Prosecutor," Clemens disciplined, "you will direct such comments to me."

"Yes, Your Honor," Barstow abdicated, "But, I must contend that..."

"Objection sustained," Clemens ended the debate.

Barstow ran his hands through his hair and tried to regroup. "Detective, will you describe the car found in the driveway at the crime scene?"

"It was a 1971 Datsun 510, white in color, with a faded blue passenger-side door," Hallstrom detailed. "The blue door was presumably a replacement from a salvage yard."

"And, Detective, is there any other evidence that would suggest that the defendant was the last person to see the victim alive?" Barstow charged.

"Yes, Sir, we found fibers on the neck of the victim that match the jacket the defendant was wearing," Hallstrom advanced.

"On the victim's neck, you say?" Barstow speculated. "And what was the cause of death according to the coroner's report?"

"The victim's neck had been broken, by a severe twisting motion," Hallstrom confirmed.

Barstow wrapped his arm around his own neck and grabbed his wrist with his other hand, imitating a choke hold around another man's neck. "Would that have been a twisting motion like this?"

Barstow violently twisted his neck around as far as he could and emitted an exaggerated grunt. That was the best performance Barstow had displayed in his hapless prosecution.

"That would be the likely way that fibers would be transferred to the victim's neck," Hallstrom surmised.

Sarah was keeping a steady watch on Josh. He purposely looked at no one. Sarah noticed a glaze over his eyes that she had not seen before. It appeared as if he wasn't even there. He was someplace else, looking for Ben.

"And about the gunshots heard, Detective, do you have any evidence regarding a weapon?" Barstow pursued.

"There were two .38 caliber slugs found," Hallstrom reported. "One was found in a wall stud, and the other had penetrated the ceiling and lodged in the attic."

"So, Detective, we can safely assume there were two gunshots?" Barstow tried to reclaim his supposition.

"Yes, Sir, ballistics confirmed that the slugs had been recently fired."

"Now, Detective," Barstow was now recharged. "I understand the weapon has not as yet been recovered. If it was not at the crime scene, what would you presume happened to it?"

"Well, Sir," Hallstrom deduced, "since no one was seen entering the house after the suspect fled, I would have to presume that the suspect took the weapon with him."

Barstow thought that this ball would go over the leftfield fence. "Would you take a gun into another man's house if you had no intention of doing harm?"

"You have to remember, Sir," Hallstrom reminded, "I wear a badge."

Oops, another foul ball into the stands. But Barstow hadn't struck out yet. At least he had gotten his point across. He couldn't afford another strike. Perhaps it was time for a bunt.

"Detective, tell me about Miss Melinda Miles."

"Melinda Miles is a twelve-year-old girl who was kidnapped ten months ago and returned home last month," Hallstrom informed.

"And," Barstow carried on. "do I understand correctly that she was returned home the same day as the murder in question?"

"That is correct," Hallstrom succinctly answered.

"And, was she the same girl the defendant identified in a photograph after his brother was killed eight months ago?" Barstow pressured.

"Yes, Sir." Hallstrom summarily disclosed.

Barstow strutted past the jury and approached the bench. "Your Honor, I would like to enter into evidence the photograph of Melinda Miles."

Barstow returned to the witness, with his chest puffed out. "Now, Detective, tell us about the identity of the murder victim."

"He had no valid identification, and he had been driving a stolen car," Hallstrom explained. "But, the Columbus Police Department provided a sketch drawn from the description the defendant gave of the assailant in his brother's death."

"And, would that then be the same man the defendant believed was holding Melina Miles captive?" Barstow attempted to confirm.

"Yes, Sir," Hallstrom concluded. "I am certain of that."

Barstow displayed the police sketch and the murder victim's photo in front of the jury. "Do you see a resemblance, ladies and gentlemen?"

"Your Honor, I offer into evidence these two pictures."

Barstow swaggered back to the witness stand, certain that this would be his game-winning grand slam.

"Help me put these pieces together, Detective. Do you think it would be reasonable to deduce that the murder victim was, in fact, the man who had been holding Melinda Miles captive, AND, that he was the man that killed the defendant's brother, Ben Marshall?"

"There is no doubt in my mind, Sir." Hallstrom had to agree.

"And, do you think it would be prudent to consider the hypothesis that the defendant was carrying Melinda Miles, wrapped in a blanket, and draped over his shoulder when he fled from the murder scene?" Barstow postulated.

"I have considered that distinct possibility, Sir." Hallstrom confided.

"Now then," Barstow tried to govern, "we have one more piece to place in this puzzle. If I consider that the defendant may have brought the .38 caliber weapon to the scene, and if I consider that your description of the victim's cause of death was far from accidental, would it be preposterous to advance the theory that there were two motives in this case? One motive being the defendant's desire to rescue Melinda Miles, and the second being the defendant's premeditated plan to leave his brother's killer dead in his wake?"

"That theory has been the crux of my investigation for the past month, Sir," Hallstrom professed.

"Well, Detective, I'm sorry to say that I must agree with you, and that leaves me with one last question for you. The only witness we have not heard from is Melinda Miles."

Josh's chair screeched on the floor, as he readied himself to charge the pitcher's mound. Sarah wrapped her arms around him and nearly sat in his lap. That drew all the attention in the courtroom, with disquieted gasps.

Clemens picked up his gavel, but when he saw Sarah holding on to Josh for dear life, he chose to simply raise his hands and suggest, "Everyone just relax."

Barstow continued, and Josh gritted his teeth. "So, Detective, is there any more light that Melinda Miles could shed in this case?"

Hallstrom weighed the benefits versus the personal costs of the proposal. "If all your hypotheses and theories are correct, Sir, Melinda Miles could positively identify the victim and the defendant. She could not testify as to the actual struggle that resulted in the victim's death unless she was in the same room."

Josh stood and stole his lap from under Sarah, but Sarah hung on. "SHE DIDN'T SEE ANYTHING! YOU LEAVE HER ALONE!"

Daddy Jake dove over the railing to tackle his son back into the chair, and Clemens' gavel was banging. "Counselor, restrain your client, or I will have to remove him from the room."

Josh was seething, but Daddy had a firm lock on him. "Calm down, Son. Take it easy. We'll work this out."

"Sir," Hallstrom tried to mediate, "it's not feasible to obtain Melinda's testimony. I have spoken to her parents, and they will not allow her to appear in court." Hallstrom gave a slight nod of acquiescence in McCay's direction. "They wouldn't even allow me to talk with their daughter."

Barstow had scored one run with his logical and deductive puzzle solving, but he thought he'd better hit for an insurance run. "You know, Detective, we could have Melinda Miles subpoenaed to appear in this court."

"NO!" Josh howled. Jake had forgotten how strong his son was, and he was about to lose hold of him. "OVER MY DEAD BODY, YOU SON-OF-A-BITCH!"

"BAILIFF, HAVE THAT MAN REMOVED FROM THIS COURTROOM!" Clemens ordered. His gavel could barely be heard over the ruckus in his courtroom and Josh's caterwauling.

It took the whole family to hold Josh down, and it broke their hearts to watch the cuffs and the shackles clamp around his limbs. Josh couldn't break his chains, but he could be heard all the way out of the courtroom.

"LOCK ME AWAY, BUT YOU BASTARDS LEAVE HER ALONE!

Sarah latched herself to Josh's side, and the officers welcomed her help. Only two officers could not contain the writhing body of their do-or-die prisoner. But the love in one small woman's voice reduced Josh's rampage to something a little less than ballistic. "JOSH! LOOK AT ME JOSH! STAY WITH ME JOSH!"

There was no chance of putting the courtroom back in order that day. Clemens' final rap of the gavel adjourned the court until tomorrow. The courtroom was cleared, except for one shuddering huddle of family sobs.

McCay raced to catch Judge Clemens before he disappeared behind the unapproachable door to his chambers. "Your Honor, may we meet in your chambers, PLEASE?"

"I think that would be wise," Clemens agreed. "Mr. Barstow, in my chambers in two minutes."

Clemens sat behind his desk, trying to recuperate from the mayhem he rarely saw in his court. McCay faced-off with Barstow like two team managers who were ready to fight for their teams.

"You two had better face me," Clemens instructed, "before I have to call the bailiff in to separate you."

"Your Honor, I apologize for my client's outburst," McCay atoned, "but please understand..."

Barstow interrupted, "That was the outburst of a crazed lunatic that needs to be..."

"MR. PROSECUTOR!" Clemens scolded like a hard-core umpire. "You shut up until you learn how to play well with others."

Barstow dropped his eyes and bit his lip.

"Please understand, Your Honor," McCay restarted, "what you just witnessed is the very essence of my client. He sat through the entire proceeding without saying a word, while his fate was being determined. He has greater concerns than his own welfare. That young man would give his life for any decent human being, especially a twelve-year-old girl. He was not speaking figuratively when he said, 'Lock me away.' And he literally means, 'Over my dead body.' I only wish I had his compassion and courage."

Clemens smoothed his mustache in thought and then asked, "Mr. Barstow, do you really intend to request a subpoena of that girl?"

"Well, Your Honor, I haven't decided," Barstow backed off, "but if the girl witnessed the murder..."

"And if she did not," Clemens countered, "you will have further tortured a young girl for no appreciable gain."

"As I said, Your Honor," Barstow tried to negate, "I haven't – I had not decided."

Clemens was close to raving. "So, what you were doing was just strategizing? That's not something you do in front of a jury!" He rose to his full six feet, three inches and menaced, "That's something you do behind closed doors, like those doors behind you that I'm about to throw you through. Get out of my chambers."

Barstow obediently faced about and headed toward the exit. McCay turned the knob on the door and planned to follow Barstow out. But Clemens hailed him back. "Not you, McCay."

McCay closed the door but kept his hand on the doorknob.

Clemens looked out the window to conceal his personal conviction. He spoke as he must, "Your boy has one more chance of behaving himself. But if he steps an inch out of line..."

"I assure you, Your Honor," McCay grasped the moment, "he'll be fine."

Clemens covered his eyes with his left hand, and with his right, he waved McCay away.

McCay had one foot out the door, but Clemens halted his stride. "Phil, I wish I had that kid's guts too."

Chapter 21

Josh woke in his cell to the smell of steaming grits and the sound of the voice that had sung him to sleep. Sarah ordered, "You wouldn't eat anything last night, so I wrangled an extra portion for you this morning. And you are going to eat it all."

Josh had no choice but to obey, with a face that bore half smile and half frown. He didn't take the tray from Sarah's hands. He reached only for the spoon and dipped it in the grits. He savored the warmth of that buttery spoonful and the warmth of Sarah's wistful eyes.

"Josh, we're going back to court this morning." Sarah paused to catch a reaction.

Josh simply dipped the spoon in the grits again and waited. As soon as Sarah's lips parted for her next word, Josh slipped that spoonful of silent sharing into her mouth.

Sarah spontaneously closed her lips around that taste of love that Josh was offering, and she swallowed while Josh grinned. "Do you think you can shut me up with grits?" Sara sputtered. "I don't even like grits. But, I'll take a bite of sausage."

Sarah spoke with her mouth full of sausage, so she could get the words out before the next bite was delivered. "Uncle Phil says they're not going to call Melinda into court."

Josh panted those quick breaths when a sob is trying to escape your throat but is held back by an overriding joy. The bites came faster, and the two companions in love's embrace consumed that breakfast with the same delight they had shared over fruit and spewing cookie crumbs.

Their time together was brief and could be measured in bites. But the love could not be measured or quantified. That love would endure the last spoonful of grits that Sarah disliked, and it would endure anything the halls of justice could dish out.

The rest of the world was not included in their walk from confinement to judgment. This was their time and their space. Any walk together could be their last. Sarah pressed her fingernails into Josh's arm, and Josh was fine with that.

When Sarah and Josh entered the courtroom, the family was waiting with bated breath. As Josh passed by them, he assured, "I'm ok. Sarah's got me."

McCay believed the heartened glint in Sarah's eyes, and he knew he was ready to proceed. He trusted the courage emblazoned on Josh's face, and that's all he needed to mount a vigorous defense.

It was McCay's turn to call witnesses for the defense, but all he had was the testimony of those who had known and believed in Josh's character and devotion. He chose first the one who knew Josh's heart the most. It was his sister, Lieutenant Junior Grade Gretchen Marshall.

Gretchen took the stand with grace and humility and command. The jurors could see that her hand on the Bible was more than a civil oath. It was a pledge to uphold every word that Bible contained.

The jury could see the attentiveness and anxiousness in Josh's eyes. He had always treasured every word his sister had spoken to him and his brother. He would not miss a syllable of anything she might say, because he knew that Ben would be listening too.

A jury would expect that a sister would support her brother, out of love and loyalty. But McCay took a stab at presenting Gretchen's pious nature. "Lieutenant Marshall, how long have you been a chaplain in the United States Navy?"

"Three years, Sir," Gretchen dutifully answered.

"I see a couple of campaign ribbons on your uniform," McCay observed. "That leads me to believe that you have served in a war zone or two."

"Yes, Sir, I have," Gretchen responded, not so much with pride as with sorrow.

"Might I also presume," Mccay trod softly, "that you have encountered many service men and women who have been troubled by the conflict between their duty as warriors and their faith?"

"That is the essence of my ministry, Sir," Sarah avowed. "I grew up in the faith, and I grew up with hundreds of veterans who faced that challenge."

"Now," McCay pushed forward, "your brother, Josh is not a military veteran, but would you say he is a warrior?"

"Since the day he was born, Sir," Gretchen undeniably claimed.

"And what were Josh's battles?" McCay queried with intense interest.

Gretchen sat with her hands in her lap and her head slightly bowed. She pondered all that she knew of her brother and softly murmured, "Joshua fought the battle of Jericho."

"Excuse me, Lieutenant, what was that?" McCay wanted the jury to hear more clearly.

Gretchen raised her head and spoke to no mortal soul. She spoke as if in prayer. "I chose Josh's name when he was born. I had no idea how fitting that name would be. Joshua fought for his people, the Israelites, and he was fearless in battle. My brother, Josh fought for anyone who needed his help. His battles were the battles of the little guy."

Gretchen looked at Josh with that big sister scowl. "I told him so many times to stay out of trouble."

Gretchen turned her head toward McCay and expounded, "But trouble seemed to follow Josh because there was always a little guy somewhere that needed his help."

Gretchen bowed her head again and spoke more to herself than to anyone else. "I don't think Josh ever lost a battle, because he always fought with his heart. You couldn't hit that boy hard enough to make him stay down if he was fighting for what he thought was right."

"Thank you, Lieutenant," McCay respectfully obliged. "One more question, please. Is your brother, Josh capable of murder?"

"Objection, Your Honor," came Barstow's complaint. "The witness has no psychological expertise on which to base an opinion of the defendant's capacity for murder. Her opinion would amount to only a sister's emotional attachment to her brother."

"On the contrary, Your Honor," McCay countered. "The defense is asking for the opinion of a spiritual counselor who has been tried and proven in war zones where the battle between life and death is a struggle we can only imagine. The defense is not asking for a psychological evaluation. We are asking what Lieutenant Marshall knows about her brother's heart."

"Objection overruled. The witness may answer," Clemens opined.

Gretchen answered directly to the judge, who was anxious to hear. "I bandaged my brother's cuts and bruises, and he never cried. He took beatings he did not deserve because as long as they were beating on him, they couldn't be beating on anyone else."

Gretchen looked at the jury that would decide her brother's fate. "There is too much love in my brother to allow him to take a life unless it was in the defense of another."

Gretchen began pointing at jury members one-by-one. "Josh would give his life for you, or you, or YOU!"

She clasped her hands in front of her mouth and stared at Josh. "I know that you were not fighting for yourself. You never have. Tell them what you were fighting for, Little Brother."

"Thank you, Lieutenant Marshall," McCay extended.

McCay decided that the jury had heard all they needed to hear about who Josh was. Gretchen summed him up perfectly, and she had left that lingering question of what had happened to bring this marvelous young man before them. "No further questions, Your Honor."

Barstow apprehensively approached the witness stand to cross-examine. Gretchen had the jury in the palm of her hand, and Barstow had to choose his words carefully. "Lieutenant Marshall, wasn't the little guy that Josh was defending most often your brother, Ben?"

"Yes, Sir," Gretchen yielded, "Ben meant the world to Josh."

"There is nothing I value more than the love of family," Barstow tried to convince the jury. "And that love can be so strong as to cloud our thoughts in times of crisis. Wouldn't you agree, Lieutenant?"

"Love is the strongest force in the universe," Gretchen proclaimed.

"Was it love that prompted Josh Marshall to pick a fight in that diner in Phoenix?" Barstow challenged.

"That wasn't picking a...," Gretchen tried to defend.

"In Mr. Marshall's statement," Barstow cutoff, "he said that he led his brother, Ben into that fight and that he threw the first punch."

"But, Josh thought that Ben needed..." Gretchen tried again to protest.

"His brother was no longer in danger," Barstow pursued. "Couldn't he have avoided any further confrontation? Couldn't he have 'turned the other cheek?"

"Yes," Gretchen struggled, "but..."

"And then," Barstow attacked, "there was the tragic death of his brother, Ben for which Josh Marshall certainly did not turn the other cheek."

There was a hint of a snarl in Gretchen's voice. "DON'T YOU DARE."

Barstow showed his indignation at Gretchen's attitude. "Don't I dare what, Lieutenant? Don't I dare suggest that Josh Marshall had a vengeful side when it came to his brother?"

Gretchen rose to her feet and gripped the railing in front of the witness stand. "Don't you dare minimalize my brother, Ben's death as an excuse for vengeance."

"Whoa," Barstow exclaimed, "it appears that the Marshall family is not slow to anger."

"Even Jesus was drawn to anger when he overturned the tables of the moneychangers in the temple," Gretchen instructed.

"But Jesus didn't kill anyone," Barstow quipped. "No further questions, Your Honor."

"YOU, PURVEYOR OF HATE!" Gretchen made her words echo through the halls of justice. The wrath of God was spewing out of her. "YOU, DISTORTER OF TRUTH!"

Clemens gavel tapped once. "The witness will be seated."

"Request to redirect, Your Honor," McCay rescued.

"Go ahead, Counselor."

McKay's gentle nature convinced Gretchen to resume her composure and to retake her seat.

"I would like you to finish your thoughts, Lieutenant," McCay soothed. "What do you know about hate versus love and vengeance versus dedication?"

Gretchen closed her eyes to calm herself. "I have pictured Ben's death so many times. It is a mystery to me how Josh lived through that."

Gretchen opened her eyes and looked upward into the firmament of her faith. "Josh did not hate. Hate would have made him immediately go after that man who sent our brother to his death. It was love that sent Josh diving off the bridge and into the river after his brother."

"Vengeance is born of hate," Gretchen directed particularly toward Barstow. "Dedication is born of love," she reminded the jury. "Josh dedicated himself to finding the young girl that Ben wanted so desperately to take home."

"Jesus did not tell us to turn the other cheek," Gretchen faithfully attested. "He told us to 'offer the other cheek as well.' Josh offered all of himself to the task of finding Melinda Miles and fulfilling a promise to our brother."

"Thank you, Lieutenant Marshall, for helping us all understand a lot more," McCay wrapped up. "No further questions, Your Honor."

The jury was spellbound in silent awe of the power of Gretchen's words, her grasp of her faith and her dedication to her brother.

McCay sauntered over to have a quiet word with Sarah. What he was really doing, however, was allowing the jury's awe to simmer a while and then gel in their minds.

Gretchen was excused from the witness stand and proceeded back to the family. As she passed by Josh, no juror could miss the love she blew through the air with a kiss that landed on Josh's cheek.

Chapter 22

Judge Clemens advanced the agenda. "Mr. McCay, will you be calling your next witness?"

"Yes, Your Honor, I would like to call Ms. Sarah Langston."

Sarah didn't have all of Josh's story, but she knew and felt enough to believe in his innocence. She was not armed with all she needed to battle in Josh's defense, but she was not short of guts.

Sarah stood straight away at the call from her Uncle Phil, but she was halted by the reflexive grasp of Josh's hand on her arm. She looked at Josh with confidence and strength. "I'll be back, Josh. Just hold my seat."

This was Sarah's first experience of testifying in court, but she mounted the witness stand like a seasoned pro. "What is there to fear," she thought, "all I need to do is follow the lead of my "knight in shining armor."

McCay greeted Sarah with his "Prince Charming smile." "Ms. Langston, I need to point out to the court and to the jury why I will call you Sarah." McCay turned to Judge Clemens. "Sarah is my only niece." That raised a brow or two in the courtroom.

Then, McCay confronted Barstow. "But do not make the mistake of selling her short." That was fair-enough warning to his opponent.

To the jury, McCay boasted with pride, "Sarah graduated from Baylor University at the top of her class."

Phil turned back to Sarah to ensure that he followed the acceptable protocol for questioning a witness. "Would you please inform the court of the degree you earned at Baylor?"

"I received a Bachelor's Degree in Psychology," Sarah modestly apprised.

"Then," Phil continued to steer the conversation, "you furthered your education at the University of Texas at Austin. Is that correct?"

Sarah dutifully answered, "Yes, that's where I completed my Master's Degree in Criminal Psychology."

"And you haven't stopped learning yet, have you Sarah?" Phil prompted.

"No, Sir, never," Sarah proudly professed. "I'm working on my dissertation, after which I will receive my Doctorate Degree in Forensic Psychology from the University of Texas at Dallas."

McCay briefly observed the jaw-dropping awe on the faces in the jurors' box. He believed that he had sufficiently accredited his witness, but still felt he could honestly and affectionately address her. "Sarah, I have always wanted to ask you what fascinates you about crime and forensics?"

Sarah sat back comfortably and smiled at Uncle Phil. He knew the answers to his question, but she was happy to tell him again. "The so-called criminal mind is the least understood among those displaying aberrant behavior."

"Some people are born with a predisposition to certain mental disorders, but no one is born with a criminal mind. There are certainly always other factors in play."

"Criminal activity is a learned behavior, and the fact that we don't fully understand it is the reason that more than half of released inmates are rearrested within five years. We cannot pretend to rehabilitate offenders without a better understanding of them."

"I knew that tuition money was well spent," McCay joked and got his snicker from the jury.

"Now, Sarah," Uncle Phil got down to business, "you have spent dozens of hours with Josh Marshall in the last few weeks. What was your first impression of him?"

Sarah slapped her hand over her mouth to stifle a laugh. "I thought he looked like a mad dog as they were dragging him through the hallway in chains."

Sarah looked at the jury and shared, "But there was something in those eyes that said, 'I don't belong here.'" She looked back at her Uncle and apologized, "That's not a very professional summation, but that was my first impression."

"And now," McCay elicited, "what is your professional summation of Josh Marshall?"

To the casual eye, it might have appeared that Sarah was unsettled and unsure, as she reviewed her prepared remarks. Actually, she was considering the value of all her clinical expertise and all the psychological jargon she had planned to present. None of it would help the jury or anyone else understand Josh Marshall. She laid her papers aside and spoke to Josh.

"There is so much more that I want to know about you, but you stopped talking, Josh. What am I supposed to tell these people? All I can tell them is that I've never met anyone like you."

Josh couldn't even look at Sarah. He covered his face with his hands, and his torso shook in helplessness.

"It's ok, Josh. Please, I didn't mean to make you cry. We have both cried enough."

Sarah turned toward the jury with conviction and steadfast resolve. "All of us are torn between competing desires and motives. 'Should I take that job promotion? How would it affect my family?' 'I really wish I could tell my in-laws what I think of them, but I don't want to hurt my spouse.' 'That jerk next door makes me so mad I could kill him, but I won't, because I don't want to go to jail.'"

"Those thoughts do not go through Josh Marshall's mind," Sarah imparted. "There is no competition between his desires and motivations. He is driven by only one force, deep in his heart. Love is his only desire and his only motive for anything he does."

"The psychological definition of unconditional love is a state of mind in which one has the goal of increasing the welfare of another, despite any evidence or benefit for oneself. Josh is the epitome of unconditional love."

Jake, Cassie, and Gretchen were Sarah's next audience. She looked at them, wanting to know, "How do you teach that much love?"

Sarah closed her eyes and bowed her head. She was now speaking to Someone above all these earthy judges and jurors and prosecutors. "I know that Josh is incapable of murder, but I know that he is capable of doing anything to protect his family. That family included Melinda Miles, whom Ben wanted to take home."

Sarah returned to her Uncle Phil's gaze and concluded, "Josh asked me twice to walk away from all of this and let him rot in jail." Sarah could scarcely gather enough breath to finish. "I guess that – that makes me – part - part of his family too."

The family was clinging to every word that came from deep within the heart of this amazing creature. It had to be obvious to the most callous observer that they wanted to wrap her into their fold. Josh was no longer the stoic figure he had maintained. His feelings were not on his sleeve, they were streaming down his cheeks.

Uncle Phil crossed the room and leaned on the rail of the jurors' box with his head low, and his shoulders slumped. He looked up with only his eyes and saw juror numbers two, five, and nine touching their tissues and handkerchiefs to their eyes. Juror number eleven shifted in his chair and didn't know what to do with his hands. Juror number seven cleared his throat, pretending it was just a tickle making him cough.

Phil was sure that Sarah had given the jury all they needed to know who Josh was. He dreaded the cross-examination of Barstow, but it was time to watch his Fair Princess do battle with the dragon. "No further questions, Your Honor, and thank you, Sarah."

Phil sauntered to his seat and sat erect, ready to watch the impending altercation. Barstow approached the witness stand, shaking his head in disappointment. "Ms. Langston, with your educational credentials presented to the court, I expected that we might hear expert testimony on the defendant's mental capacity and predispositions. But I didn't hear any psychological evidence that would refute the possibility of the defendant being a psychotic killer, a schizophrenic out of control, or just a vengeful psychopath. All I heard was a young woman who is in love with her patient."

"Objection, Your Honor," McCay demanded. "I'm waiting to hear a question from the prosecution, rather than his own opinion."

"Mr. Barstow," Clemens instructed, "proceed with your question."

Barstow was unabashed and proceeded in his cold-hearted, prosecutorial tone, "Ms. Langston, do you have any 'empirical' evidence as to the defendant's propensity for lethal violence?"

All emotion fell from Sarah's face. Barstow had thrown down the gauntlet at her feet, and she was more than willing to pick it up. McCay had seen that look before and grinned in anticipation. Sarah was going to take the gloves off for this fight.

"Mr. Prosecutor," she boldly retorted. "you threw out a few terms that are loosely used interchangeably by the uninformed. I will answer them one-by-one, and you may want to take notes."

Sarah paused for the faint chuckle coming from a few jurors. "Schizophrenia is characterized by abnormal social behavior, a failure to understand what is real, false beliefs, confused and unclear thinking, anxiety, depression, and lack of motivation."

Sarah spoke to the jury to affirm, "None of those characteristics describe Josh Marshall." She looked back at Barstow and finished round one. "And a lack of 'motivation' could be construed as a lack of motive."

Barstow was starting to wish that he had stayed in his corner of the ring. "Yes, well, Ms. Langston, let's move on..."

"I'm not finished answering all of your questions," Sarah relentlessly pounded.

"Your Honor, please," Barstow implored.

"The witness may continue to answer 'all' of the questions," Clemens opined. "Are you taking notes, Mr. Barstow?"

"If you want to lump all abnormal behavior into one label," Sarah accused, "the most accurate would be Antisocial Personality Disorder. Those suffering from this disorder, and I emphasize 'suffering,' typically have no regard for right and wrong. Josh Marshall cared enough to offer his life for right over wrong."

"You used the term psychopath," Sarah continued the attack." Barstow had no excuse for not nodding in confession.

"It is common for the terms psychopath and sociopath to be used interchangeably, but they are very different disorders," Sarah lectured.

She was done shutting Barstow down. She now owned the jury and spoke and articulated only to them, "A psychopath lacks emotion, empathy, remorse, and guilt. You saw and heard the emotion screaming out of Josh as they drug him from the courtroom. You heard his empathy for a young girl as he begged the court to lock him away but leave Melinda Miles alone. You witnessed the selfless courage of a man willing to accept all guilt and all punishment, even including the loss of his mortal life."

Barstow could not handle the beating his case was taking. "Your Honor, I must object!"

Clemens waved away Barstow's interruption. "Be quiet, Mr. Prosecutor. I'm taking notes."

Repressing a grin, Sarah continued. "Sociopaths, when confronted, make it clear that they couldn't care less about how others feel. They can be considered hotheaded by nature. Now, yes, you have me there. Josh Marshall is a hot-head anytime someone threatens or defames his family. Aren't we all?"

"Psychopaths are skilled actors who will persist, believing themselves to be superior to others. They are more typically described as cold-hearted." Sarah shrugged her shoulders and added, "Those qualities could possibly assist them in being a prosecuting attorney."

There were too many laughs, and Barstow knew there was no use in trying to object over Judge Clemens' snicker.

"Sociopaths recognize other people's distress even as they try to rationalize their own actions. Psychopaths do not. Violence, while possible, is not an inherent characteristic of either psychopathy or sociopathy."

"Thank you, Ms. Langston, I believe you have answered all my questions," Barstow tried to escape.

"All but one, Sir," Sarah maintained the upper hand.

Barstow surrendered the floor and sank hopelessly into his chair.

"It is not true that I am in love with my patient." Sarah denied.

The entire courtroom watched the color drain out of Josh's face. Uncle Phil's eyebrows rose into the wrinkles of his forehead. Jake and Cassie locked their white knuckles together. Only Gretchen knew where this was going.

"Josh ceased to be my patient after the first day I knew him," Sarah confessed without regret. "He is my friend, and I hope he trusts that I will always be his friend. I am his professional confidante, but even I have not been allowed to know what we all need to know. WHAT HAPPENED ON THAT TERRIBLE DAY?"

Sarah could calm herself only by looking deep into Josh's eyes. "I know why you haven't told me. You're trying to protect everyone from some awful truth, but you can't bear it alone. I won't let you. And I will never give up on you or on us."

For Sarah, there was only Josh and herself left in the courtroom. "You know I love you, Dummy." Josh's face looked as if it was going to melt away. "I love who you are, and I love what we are. And I can only dream about what we could be."

Sarah's sojourn into the possibilities of the future was all too brief. She could not escape the reality of the present. In a final appeal to the jury, Sarah explained one more psychological phenomenon.

"In a 1986 paper, Robert Sternberg proposed the triangular theory of love." Judge Clemens picked up his pencil to take more notes.

"In Sternberg's model, all love is composed of one or more of three elements: intimacy, passion, and commitment. Those are not simply terms for physical attraction. You can be intimate with your best friend and share your biggest secrets. You can be passionate about your job or about a cause. You can be committed to an ideal or committed to the welfare of another."

"Using different combinations of these elements, Sternberg described eight different kinds of love. The ultimate kind of love contains all three elements, and he called that 'consummate love.' That is the kind of love you get from Josh Marshall."

"The only thing Josh can be accused of is loving too much. BUT THERE IS NO SUCH THING!"

Sarah had given all she had to give, at least for now. "I think I'm finished, Uncle Phil."

"May the witness step down? "Uncle Phil requested.

"No further questions," Barstow backed down.

Sarah rejoined her Josh. She tried to sit in a refined, professional manner. She resisted the overwhelming urge to embrace her Sweetheart. But, she did not resist Josh's hand that enveloped hers.

Chapter 23

No one could attest to Josh's character as well as Gretchen and Sarah had defined. And none could provide any facts that would help to exonerate McKay's client. All the facts were locked inside Josh's impenetrable will. But McKay trudged on to his next witness.

"Your Honor, I would like to call to the witness stand Sergeant Gabriel Sandoval."

Gabe stood with honor and approached the witness stand as a privilege. He was sworn in and gave the oath that he gave every day he put on his uniform. They were not just words to him, they were a code by which he lived.

"Sergeant Sandoval," McKay respectfully greeted, "I understand that you knew Josh and Ben Marshall very well."

"Yes, Sir, better than most," Gabe wagered.

"Please tell us, Sergeant, how did you come to know them."

The corners of Gabe's eyes crinkled in a smile. "I watched them grow up at "Eddie's Place.""

"So, you were one of the many returning Vietnam vets who found solace at Eddie's Place," McKay lead on.

"Yes, Sir. I was one of the lucky ones who found a home and a family that gave me what I needed after that war had taken away everything I had." Gabe's eyes were tearing, but his face was set like stone.

"So," McKay surmised, "Josh and Ben were like family to you."

"No, Sir," Gabe wagged his head, "they were not "like" family. They "were" family. Watching those boys grow up helped all the vets return to their childhood. Watching them work side-by-side with us made us all work harder. Watching the brotherhood between them gave us all hope that we would find that kind of love again."

McKay removed his handkerchief from his breast pocket and dabbed his eyes. His tears were real, and he folded them back into his pocket. "Thank you, Sergeant. Now, I need to ask you about the incident in Phoenix. Were you one of the police officers responding to a call regarding a fight at the "Sunrise Diner?"

"Yes, Sir. By Divine Providence, I was." Gabe looked at Gretchen for her confirmation, and Gretchen touched the cross of Jesus on her lapel.

McKay progressed to the pertinent facts that Barstow had used to defame Josh. "Were you able to determine who started that fight in the diner, Sergeant Sandoval?"

"Every witness statement I reviewed convinced me that the other two truck drivers started the fight," Gabe swore.

"I see," McKay responded. "That is – well- no, Sergeant, I don't see. I'm confused. Josh stated that he threw the first punch. Wouldn't that suggest that Josh was the one who instigated the violence?"

"That's not what started the fight," Gabe clarified. "The other truck driver blew smoke in Ben's face. He flicked ashes in his plate. He dropped his cigarette butt in Ben's coffee. He bullied a relatively defenseless human being. I define that as violence."

"Thank you, Sergeant, I think I understand now," Mckay concluded. "No further questions Your Honor."

Barstow was not satisfied with Gabe's answer, and in his cross-examination, he would challenge Gabe's assertion. "Sergeant Sandoval, I'm afraid I still don't understand that first punch. It seems to me that the truck drivers started the confrontation, but the defendant was the one who started the fisticuffs."

Gabe looked hard at Barstow and wondered whether he had ever been in battle in defense of a brother. "Have you ever heard of a retaliatory strike, Mr. Prosecutor?"

"Of course," Barstow answered with indignance, "retaliation is synonymous with revenge. That supports my opinion that the defendant acted only out of a desire to avenge the wrong against his brother."

"The purpose of a retaliatory strike is not to exact revenge," Gabe corrected. "The purpose of a swift retaliation is to let the enemy know that an attack on your brother will not go unpunished, and they had better not do it again. Josh Marshall can take a punch and brush it off. But if you attack his brother or sister, he will not let it lie."

"So," Barstow spitefully argued, "when the defendant murdered the man who had killed his brother, you would prefer to call that retaliation?"

"Objection, Your Honor. The witness has no knowledge of the homicide under investigation," McKay blasted.

"Objection sustained," Clemens quickly ordered.

Barstow's question would be stricken from the record, but Gabe decided to finish this particular fight. "Retaliation would have been useless. Josh no longer had a brother to defend. Whatever happened in Plano, I can guarantee you it could not be retaliation. If you don't understand that, Mr. Barstow, then you are not capable of understanding Josh Marshall, and you are not worthy to be in his presence."

"Your Honor," Barstow tried to plead.

"Do you have any further questions of the witness, Mr. Barstow?" Clemens interceded.

Barstow took his lumps again and submitted, "No Your Honor, no further questions."

Gabe paused on his way back to the gallery to touch the collective hands of Jake, Cassie, and Gretchen and quietly promised, "I'll see you next Thanksgiving."

McKay decided that Barstow had been beaten down enough that it was time for Josh to take him on. "Your Honor, I would like to call to the stand the defendant, Josh Marshall."

The jury was entranced, in anticipation of hearing from this extraordinary young man. All of them wanted to believe. All of them wanted to hear the secret that he guarded with his life.

Would Josh tell the truth? Maybe some. Would he tell the whole truth? Never. Would he tell nothing but the truth? Always.

Josh kissed Sarah's hand and reluctantly rose. He turned to face his father, who had taught him courage and gave a nod of fearlessness. He mimicked a smooch to his mother, who had nurtured him in love. He winced when he looked at Gretchen and wagged his head in apology for not being all that she had taught him to be.

Josh took the stand and sat as rigid as a statue. He was ready for any question, but he was not ready for every answer.

"Josh," McCay strategically feigned, "I want you to know that you are the most trying and difficult client I have ever represented."

Josh had no response and no visible reaction. Josh heard every word that invaded his ears, but he wasn't really present in that courtroom. He was listening and searching for Ben.

"Josh, did you not tell me that you didn't need a lawyer and that I was fired?" McCay elicited.

"Yes Sir." Josh solemnly answered.

"And why did you do that, Josh?"

Josh's eyes darted to the jury, and then his family, and then to his love. "Because I don't care what happens to me."

The jury audibly choked and wanted to know why. Sarah covered her face and sobbed, "Oh, JOSH, NO!"

"How could you not care, Josh," McCay egged on. "I know that you have a loving family to go home to. I know that you are in love with my niece. How can you not care?"

For the first time in many months, Josh totally broke, with no more will to fight. His shoulders and limbs became useless, and he sobbed like a brotherless child. His head careened forward and struck the railing of the witness stand, and he rolled his head back and forth along the railing.

McCay was sorry that he had called Josh to the witness stand. It felt like the worst decision he had ever made. "Your Honor, I would like to request a recess."

"NOooo!" Josh petitioned. He sat up erect and directed, "Get this over with." Josh faced the jury and implored, "Make your decision. Let me live or let me die. I DON'T CARE!"

Everyone in the courtroom could hear Gretchen's Heavenly plea, "There is no greater love than this."

"Your Honor, PLEASE, grant us a recess!" Mcay pleaded.

"Your Honor," Barstow seized the opportunity, "the defendant has expressed a desire to continue."

McCay was seething, but Josh stepped up to the challenge. He leveled his head so that one eye could keep a watch on his opponent, Barstow, while the other eye relayed a vow to his defender. "Let him ask his questions, Uncle Phil."

Uncle Phil leaned in and saw the conviction in Josh's eyes. That was exactly what he needed to see. It was the fire and the resolve that he knew Josh possessed. He saw a young man who was ready to do battle and Uncle Phil stepped aside. "No further questions, Your Honor."

Barstow approached the witness stand, certain that this would be his game-winning run. "Mr. Marshall, isn't it true that you have never stated a denial of killing the man in this photograph?"

Josh was fixed on Sarah and saw her echo Uncle Phil's nod of affirmation. "It is better to remain silent," Josh quoted, "and be thought a fool than to speak and to remove all doubt. Abraham Lincoln."

The jury chuckled in anticipation of which fool would speak next and Barstow realized that Josh had thrown the first pitch right at his chin. But he shook it off and stepped a little further back from the plate. "Without a denial, I must assume that you did kill this man."

Josh threw another inside pitch. "Your assumptions are your windows on the world. Scrub them off every once in a while, or the light won't come in. Isaac Asimov."

Judge Clemens was trying desperately not to laugh and shielded his face from view. The jurors held their chuckles inside, but they could be seen in their jiggling bodies. Josh's family was uplifted and revitalized to see their boy back in the game. Uncle Phil looked at the glow in Sarah and whispered, "If I can get this young man acquitted, I just may give him a job."

Barstow was pounding his bat on Homeplate, wishing this kid would throw him something he could hit. "I see that you're not just a dumb truck driver, Mr. Marshall. I had been told, however, that you are a cocky young man."

McCay withheld his objection to this slanderous remark and listened for Josh's response. "Never enter a battle of wits half-armed. William Shakespeare."

No one in the courtroom could hold back their raucous laughter. Even Judge Clemens could not keep a straight face, but he gave a few obligatory raps of the gavel until the cackling quieted.

Barstow had thrown his bat in the dirt and shouted, "You don't understand how serious your situation is! Don't you know that you are in a fight for your life?"

"I have feared only one thing in my life," Josh pronounced.

Barstow didn't want to give Josh another shot at him and ignored Josh's proclamation, but Josh finished it off anyway. "The only thing I ever feared in my life was a good whuppin' from my Daddy."

Jake and Cassie were beaming with joy and pride. Gretchen looked upward and burst out "HALLELUJAH!"

Barstow's composure was now obliterated, and he exploded in a charge toward the pitcher's mound. "DID YOU, OR DID YOU NOT KILL THE MAN IN THIS PHOTOGRAPH?"

Josh looked at his Daddy, Jake, and said, "I deserved every one of those whuppins, and they made me who I am today."

He spoke to his Momma, Cassie. "I was wrong to deny my heritage, and I'm sorry for turning my back on the family that means everything to me."

He petitioned Gretchen's forgiveness. "I was confused when I lost faith in Ben's love. That love did not die that awful early morning. You taught me that."

"Mr. Marshall," Barstow ranted, "you need to answer my question."

Josh gave Barstow that look he always gave any time he spread his feet into his fighting stance. "I'll let you know when I'm finished."

"Your Honor," Barstow appealed, "would you please instruct the witness…"

"Mr. Barstow," Clemens overrode, "I believe the witness is instructing you. I suggest that you listen."

Josh finally spoke his heart to Sarah. "If love should ever come my way again, I will know that love is filled with happiness and woe. That won't stop me. My heart will still go out because that's what love is all about. Love doesn't care how long it shall live. It only cares about how much it can give."

Josh turned back to Barstow to let him know that he was finished. "You can't do anything to me, and my family does not deserve this. I have said all that I am going to say."

Josh stood and stepped down from the witness stand. He ignored Clemens' gavel and his command, "The defendant will return to the stand."

Josh halted half-way back to Sarah, as she pushed her palms forward, motioning Josh back to the stand. Josh stood between Heaven and hell. He had many times made the wrong choice. This time, there was only one choice he could make. He turned to face Judge Clemens. "Your Honor, I would like to change my plea to…"

From the very rear of the gallery, a young girl burst through the swinging gate of oak and scrambled into Josh's arms. Josh hugged back with equal passion and held her head to his chest, with his fingers woven through the soft blonde curls.

The onlookers gasped in wonderment and awe, and McCay sighed in visible and audible relief. "Your Honor, I would like to introduce Miss Melinda Miles."

Barstow was too astonished to object to any improper procedure and doubted that such would be sustained.

Melinda raised her head and stared into Josh's eyes. "You came for me, and now I have come for you. I didn't know your name, I just knew your brother's name, because I heard you call it out."

"How did you find me, Punkin?" Josh endeared.

"My Mom has been reading about your trial, and yesterday, she showed me your picture. I said, THAT'S HIM, MOM! WE'VE GOT TO GO THERE!"

Josh stroked those curls again. "How have you been, Punkin?"

Melinda's eyes lit up like candles on the cake. "Oh, today is my 13th birthday!"

Josh laughed, and the courtroom cheered. Handkerchiefs and tissues were shared, and hearts were joined in a chorus of love.

"Guess what, Josh," Melinda tempted.

"What, Punkin?" Josh invited.

"Ben wished me a happy birthday too, Josh."

All those singing hearts were shocked and spellbound, most of which was Josh's. Josh dropped to his knees and quivered in incredulous anticipation. He held Melinda's hand to his lips. "You heard him?"

"I heard him in my dream, Josh, and he told me to tell you something."

Josh couldn't speak, and he didn't have to. His plea could be seen in the tear streaming down his cheek.

Melinda collected that tear on the tip of her finger and smiled with the angels. "Ben said that you should have eaten his Twinkie."

A collective gasp rolled through the courtroom. It wasn't hard to believe this innocent revelation, it was impossible not to believe. Josh's head was buried in Melinda's embrace, and she laid her face in his hair. From deep within that embrace, a sound invaded Josh's ears.

"*Josh?*"

Josh gently unwrapped himself from Melinda's arms and looked all around the courtroom. All eyes followed his gaze, but no one could see what Josh heard.

"*Josh?*"

Josh's eyes flashed upwards and his face melted into rapture. "Yeah, Ben?"

Everyone in the courtroom instinctively looked up at the ceiling for the object of Josh's ecstasy. There was nothing to be seen, it could only be heard in Josh's voice.

"Yeah, Ben?"

"*It's time to tell them, Josh.*"

The fascinated spectators got to hear only Josh's side of the conversation, but that's all they needed to hear.

"Ok, Ben, what do I say?"

"*Say what Gretchen taught us, Josh. Tell them what we were fighting for.*"

Josh buttressed his will and swore to his brother, "Ok, Ben. I'll tell them. I promise. Thank you, Ben. Stay with me Ben. Stay right behind me."

"*Ok, Josh. I will.*"

Josh squared his shoulders for the fight. He looked at Melinda with the confidence of love. "I'm going to have to get you a birthday present later, Punkin. Now, I need you to go back to your parents while I attend to some business."

Josh lifted Melinda with her arms encircling his neck. He carried her back to her parents and received the handshake of a father and the hug of a mother.

"Thank you for bringing our baby home," Mr. Miles' voice broke.

"God bless you," Mrs. Miles graced.

Josh turned to Sarah. "I'm ready to tell you everything, Sarah. Will you help me with the words?" Sarah nodded with all of her being, keeping her eyes fixed on her mighty warrior.

McCay clenched the appeal. "Your Honor, I request a recess so that my client can prepare the rest of his statement."

Clemens waited a moment for any possible objection from the prosecution. Barstow could only raise his hands in surrender.

Chapter 24

The court was recessed for two hours, and Sarah and Josh were alone once more. There were no handcuffs, no bars, and no guards watching. For the first time, they could embrace with all their love and share a long-awaited kiss. Sarah broke the kiss with a finger on Josh's lips. "We have work to do."

Sarah sat with her pad and pen as she always had, ready to record every moment she had longed to hear. Josh sat as he had not for a very long time. There was pride in his posture and courage in his voice. There was no longer regret in his words. He knew now that Ben was right behind him.

Sarah wrote in an unrestrained frenzy and marveled at the fire that was back in Josh's eyes. The words were not easy for the speaker or the listener, but they flowed from Josh's mouth to Sarah's pad in a torrent of purpose.

Josh divulged secrets he thought he would never disclose. But he was doing what Ben had asked him to do. He was speaking as a whole person again.

Sarah heard once unspeakable horrors and undaunted courage. She heard about intimacy and passion and commitment. She heard the definition of consummate love.

When the last agonizing fact had been spoken, and Sarah had written the last heartbreaking word, she grabbed the face of her heart's desire. "You did it, Josh. You did it!"

"No, My Love," Josh set right, "we did it, you, me and Ben."

Sarah flung the door open and announced, "We're ready."

The court was reconvened at a moment's notice. No one, including The Honorable Judge Clemens, could wait to hear the rest of the story.

"Your Honor," McCay introduced, "we did not delay these proceedings with printing and copying. I ask that Ms. Sarah Langston be allowed to read the remainder of my client's statement, to which he has attested."

"She may proceed, Counselor."

Sarah stood at the small podium and prefaced Josh's testimony with her own confession. "Your Honor, Ladies, and Gentlemen of the Jury, I am indeed in love with Josh Marshall, and I think you have been exposed to ample reasons why."

"I also love and respect my profession. And this is what my profession is supposed to be about. It is about a journey, no matter how long, to discover truths buried in the heart and mind of our fellow man or woman."

"This journey began with Josh unable to utter his own name and unable to bear the shame and sorrow that haunted him. The shame is gone now, thanks to his brother, Ben Marshall. The sorrow will linger, but it will diminish, now that Josh's heart is ready to go on."

"You last read that Josh found that small white car with a blue door. He was going to return to his car and notify the police. But, Josh hesitated a second too long." Sarah read directly from her pad without adding or deleting a word. This was Josh's story, and she told it all.

By the time Josh realized that he needed to keep walking, his rising body temperature sent pheromones to the nose of a neighbor's Doberman. The dog thrust against his fenced enclosure and sounded the alarm with vicious snarls and barks.

Josh turned to run back, but the front door of the house flung open, and the eyes of evil bulged as they recognized Josh. The evil hand moved toward the pocket, and Josh knew that in three seconds or less, the muzzle of a .38 caliber gun would be pointed his way.

Josh charged at the evil, not by choice, but by reflex. The hand was deep in the pocket that held his death when Josh hit his first stride. The gun emerged from the pocket as he completed his second stride. The hammer cocked during his third stride, and a fourth stride would be his last.

Josh pushed off his right foot and lunged with his left arm outstretched, and his hand vaulted toward the gun. The gun fired as good, and evil crashed to the floor, and Melinda Miles screamed, and the Doberman barked louder.

"RUN, MELINDA!" Josh bellowed, but all Melinda could do is emit a muffled scream.

Josh had one arm around his assailant's neck and a firm grip on the wrist behind the gun, a grip hardened on the steering wheel of an 18,000-pound truck. Another shot rang out, and the neighbors were all peeking through their window blinds.

Josh's adversary was strong as a bull, but Josh had wrestled a few steers in his day. As the bull slowly and agonizingly cranked his wrist and turned the muzzle perilously close to Josh's face, Josh rolled and used all his weight to twist the neck of that steer until the vertebrae cracked.

The limp body lay heavy on top of Josh, and Josh kept his steel grip on the wrist until he had wrenched the gun out of the hand that had tortured so many lives. Josh scooted out from under the carcass and ran toward Melinda's squeals and whimpers.

He found the bedroom door locked when he rattled the knob, but three kicks with his steel-toed boot opened Melinda's prison. She was tied to the bed, gagged with a dish towel and had only the faintest slip of clothing. He leaned over the trembling body that had been ravaged and beaten for months of an eternity and promised, "I'm going to get you home, Melinda."

Melinda recognized the face she had seen and the voice she had heard on the bridge over the Chattahoochee River. Her head began to bob in a frenzy of disbelief and hope.

Josh took the gag off, and those quivering lips begged, "Who was that guy that fell into the river?"

Josh didn't slow in his efforts to unbind the arms and legs that ached and burned in torment. "That was my brother, Ben. Let's go!"

Josh wrapped the fragile young girl in a blanket, from head to toe, and lifted her onto his shoulder. A faint whimper escaped from the blanket, as Josh stepped over the dead body he would leave behind. After all her months of torture, Melinda was crying for Ben and for Josh, whose name she didn't even know.

A few neighbors had braved their fears and emerged from their homes. They saw Josh barreling over the lawn and across the street with his precious parcel. He laid the sobbing bundle in the back seat. "You're on your way home, Punkin."

The bravest of neighbors were closing in on him, but before Josh even got the door of the car closed, he switched on the ignition, slammed the transmission into gear, and buried the gas pedal under his foot.

Any sane man would have stopped and called for help. Any clear-thinking person would have called the authorities and told their story. But Josh didn't stop to think when he dove into the Chattahoochee after Ben, he reacted as love demanded.

Love often does not allow time for clear thinking, it simply propels. Ben always acted out of love, and Josh was doing exactly what Ben would have done. The only thing that mattered at this moment was to get Melinda Miles home.

"Where is your home, Melinda? Which way do I go?"

"MURPHY!" was the answer from under the blanket. "CREEKSIDE DRIVE!"

Josh obeyed all the rules of the road and scanned every inch of the seven-mile trip to Murphy. "Keep your eyes peeled for road signs, Ben. We need to get to Murphy. I'll watch out for police cars. Ok, Ben?"

But Ben didn't answer. Josh called out to his navigator again, "Ok, Ben? BEN!"

Ben had never refused to answer his brother's plea. Was Ben mad at him for what he had done? Was Ben even there? Of course, Ben was there. He had to be. Josh couldn't imagine otherwise. "I'll get Melinda home, Ben. Trust me."

"Melinda, come up here and tell me where to turn."

Melinda cautiously, yet excitedly came out from under the blanket and slid over into the front passenger seat. She held her hands over her private parts that she hoped still belonged to her. "What is your name, Sir?"

Josh didn't answer for a minute or two, but Melinda just had to know. "Please, Sir, tell me your name."

Josh glanced at that yearning young face and then back to the road. He fondly revealed the only truth that mattered. "I am Ben's brother, and it's Ben who is taking you home."

"Turn here – take the Farm to Market Road," Melinda shrieked.

Melinda rolled the window down and took in all the smells of home. She became giddy when she saw the school of dance, where she had learned ballet and fell down every time she performed. She cried tears of joy at the sight of the gas station where the owner always treated her with a piece of bubble gum. She was already home, and she needed only one thing more, to be wrapped in the arms of Mommy and Daddy.

"Turn left here, McCreary Road!" Melinda squealed.

Melinda bounced in the seat as they passed each house and block that had filled her childhood. "CREEKSIDE DRIVE! TURN LEFT!"

Melinda kept her hand on the door handle for the next three blocks. Josh knew where to stop when Melinda yanked on the handle, and the passenger door flew open. There were no farewells, and there were no thanks needed.

Josh kept the transmission in drive and watched Melinda race up the walk to the front door. She pounded on the door with double-fisted fervor. The door opened wide, and a father's mouth flew open.

Josh waited until he saw Melinda safely encased in her Daddy's arms. Then he slammed the accelerator to the floor. His tires screeched on the pavement still covered with morning dew.

Josh had no idea where he was headed or where to turn next. He just drove. He tried again to summon his brother, "We did it Ben! We got her home. Will you talk to me now, Ben?"

Still, there was no answer. There was just Josh and the road, with the telephone poles zipping by.

"There's a sign for Bethany Lakes Park. How about we go there, Ben? Ben? Oh, Ben, please, you've got to talk to me."

"What are we going to do when we get there, Ben?" Josh needed his brother more now than he ever had. He had never been in this much trouble without Ben by his side.

Josh followed the signs and parked near the lake. He shut the engine down and collapsed against the steering wheel. "Oh, Ben, I know I shouldn't have run. I should've gone straight to the police. I didn't want to kill that man. You know that, don't you, Ben?"

Josh had never known silence in his life, and he had never fathomed how deafening that silence could be. He took off his gloves and reached in his pocket for his handkerchief, to daub his tears.

His fingers fumbled over the hard steel of the .38 revolver. He withdrew the gun and stared in earthshaking horror. "Oh, Ben, I'm in a lot of trouble."

Josh shivered for hours in sheer fear. He prayed, he pleaded, and he called out Ben's name. "WHERE ARE YOU, BEN? WHERE ARE YOU, GOD?"

The sun rose to the highest point in its arc, and Josh's tears were mixed with sweat. The sun set, and darkness fell hard on a desperate young man who was all alone.

Josh reluctantly accepted his lonely fate. He gathered all the resolve that was left in him. He made the choice he had always made.

"Don't worry, Ben. I'll take care of this. I'll take the blame, and I won't tell anyone that I'm your brother. If you're gone, then so am I. Without you, I don't exist."

Josh got out of the car and walked to the shore of the lake. He hurled the revolver into the deepest water it could reach. He took out his wallet and lit a match to take one last look at Ben's picture. It wasn't just Ben in the picture. It never was. Ben was perched on top of Josh's shoulders, and that smile was what Josh had lived for.

Then, identification, memories, and every dollar Josh had to his name followed the same course as the gun.

Josh lumbered back to the car, picking up the largest stones he could find along the way. He started the engine and smashed the parking brake to the floor. He shifted the automatic transmission into drive, and the hard-locked brake resisted the push of the crankshaft. Josh piled stones against the accelerator, one-by-one until the engine was turning over 700 rpm.

The car started creeping forward, and Josh jumped out onto his feet. He reached back in to grasp the parking brake release handle and pulled, sending himself to his butt. He watched the car disappear in the dark, murky water. He no longer owned a car. He no longer had a brother. He no longer possessed a name.

But that did not erase the responsibility Josh deeply felt. He had to go back. He had to face the music. That is what he had always done. And maybe, just maybe, that would be enough for Ben to forgive him.

Josh raised his empty shell to an upright stance, turned the collar up on his jacket and buttoned the top button. He crossed his arms, buried his hands in his armpits, and wished he hadn't left his gloves in the car.

He turned toward Plano and began to walk. He walked to ward off the cold. He walked to numb his mind. He wasn't going to run away. He'd never known how. He walked for an hour and forty-five minutes, back to the scene of the crime.

Flashlights and headlights illuminated the lawn of the house from which he had extracted that beautiful young girl and left death in his wake. The flashing of red and blue had brought curious gawkers from blocks away.

Josh didn't hesitate or break his stride. He ducked under the yellow police tape and marched on.

A police officer shined a flashlight in the face of this trespasser, and a woman behind the yellow tape yelled, "THAT'S HIM! That's the killer that ran away!"

That was not quite all of Josh's statement, but that was all that Sarah got to read. From the midst of the courtroom gallery, a voice of conviction shouted, "YOUNG JOSH NEVER RUN AWAY. HE ALWAYS RUN TO!"

All eyes were directed to a small man of great courage and limitless love. Jake shot out of his chair like a projectile and called out, "Hi-Hi!"

Jake sailed over Cassie into the crowd and grabbed the old man he had cherished since his youth. He clung to everything that was made possible by this selfless man. The crowd was in such a rumpus, Clemens' gavel was banging again for order in his court.

Josh leapt from his seat to join in the hug and Cassie and Gretchen could not be held back. They had all dreamed of someday seeing and touching this man who was the impetus of an entire, grateful family.

No one paid attention to the bashing of the gavel, and Clemens shouted above the din, "BAILIFF, CLEAR THE COURTROOM!"

The bailiff approached the bench, so he could speak without yelling. "Your Honor, I think I would have to call the National Guard."

The bailiff had been watching out the window of the courtroom and walked over to the television in the corner to switch on Channel 5.

"Ladies and gentlemen, we are bringing you scenes from outside the Dallas Federal Court Building," the newscaster projected into his microphone.

The cameras panned the sea of humanity trailing down the courthouse steps, across the street, and spreading out over the lawn, as the newscaster continued. "These people have been gathering here all morning. The nearest we can estimate is that there are more than three hundred people here, and they are still coming. They have come to support Mr. Josh Marshall, who is on trial for murder. They have come by every mode of transportation imaginable, some even walking many miles."

The camera zoomed in on some of the most notable members of this rag-tag army, and the newscaster pointed out, "I am struck by how many have come on crutches and in wheelchairs. One man, with no legs, is riding on the back of a brother. Most of them are military veterans, and they all know each other from a farm in Hayes, Kansas, called "Eddie's Place.""

The newscaster moved close to Sam and introduced, "This man says he has known Josh Marshall all of the young man's life."

Sam made sure his voice was heard over the microphone. "I was there when he was born. He taught me more than I ever taught him. There isn't a mean bone in that man's body, but he fears nothing that walks. If there was a fight, he didn't start it, but he could sure as hell finish it."

Brenda commandeered the microphone and proclaimed, "Josh has always been a hero, and they had better give him back to us."

The newscaster could no longer be heard when he tried to sign off with his name and TV station identification. His microphone became useless to him against the clamor of chanting. "GIVE JOSH BACK! GIVE JOSH BACK!"

Dozens of feet in the courtroom were stomping in rhythm with the chant. Even Judge Clemens' gavel rapped to that same beat.

Clemens motioned a directive for the bailiff to turn off the TV. All seats were taken, and the cheering in the courtroom slowly subsided into some semblance of order.

"Well," The Honorable Judge Clemens surmised, "it appears that the defense neglected to call a few character witnesses." Everyone chortled and nodded.

"But I think they have all spoken," Clemens opined. "May we proceed, Please?"

"Your Honor," McKay petitioned, "I would like to call one more witness who has just arrived. I call Mr. Hi-Hi Nyugen."

Clemens looked at Barstow out of respect for the due process of law. Barstow no longer had a reason or the desire to object.

Hi-Hi bowed his way out of all the embraces and humbly approached the witness stand. With a bit of trepidation, he climbed the steps and placed his hand on the bible. He looked directly at no one, which was his custom. His oath was that of a man who had chosen to be an American.

"Mr. Nyugen," McKay greeted.

"Hi-Hi, please," Mr. Nyugen murmured.

"Excuse me, what was that, Mr. Nyugen?"

"I am called Hi-Hi."

"Very well, Hi-Hi, if you will call me Phil."

"Happy to meet you, Phil."

"Do I understand correctly that you were a soldier in the North Vietnamese Army, an enemy of the United States?"

Hi-Hi only bowed his head in acknowledgment.

Phil took a gamble. "What was your most memorable day in the war you experienced?"

Hi-Hi's head was still bowed, but he raised a finger to point toward Jake. "Young man. Tied to tree. Starved. Beaten."

"Your Honor, may the court record note that the witness is pointing to the defendant's father, Jake Marshall, who was a prisoner of war in North Vietnam?"

"It will be so noted," Clemens guaranteed.

"And, Hi-Hi," McKay coaxed, "I understand that you set that young man free."

"No," Hi-Hi denied, "I cut him loose, but I set me free. He run back to his family, and I run away from mine." No one knew the magnitude of Hi-Hi's admission. He had left a home and family behind, not so much for a better life, but for a better ideal.

"And now, Hi-Hi, are you an American citizen?" McCay wanted every American to know.

Hi-Hi raised his head to let his pride show. "YES! I study English. I study American History. I take test. I am now an American!"

"Welcome to America, Hi-Hi," Phil graciously appreciated.

Phil paused to look at the faces in the jury and assure himself that they were accepting this new, proud American citizen. Phil then laid his arms on the railing of the witness stand and rested his chin on his hands, like a curious and expectant lad who wanted to hear more of the story.

"How did you know that Josh Marshall was the son of that young man you cut loose?" Phil spurred on.

"Eyes," Hi-Hi swiftly answered. "He have father's eyes. I never forget eyes."

"And what was your impression of "Young Josh?" Phil induced.

"He work hard," Hi-Hi attested. "He learn cash register. He sweep and mop. He keep shelves neat. He never ask for anything. He just work."

"And didn't Young Josh show you the picture of the young girl, Melinda Miles?" Phil got to the meat of his questions.

"YES!" Hi-Hi affirmed. "He show me picture of beautiful young girl who in trouble." Hi-Hi was now near tears.

"He show me drawing of man with eyes I never forget. I tell him I see this man. I tell him this man have girl. I tell him about white car with blue door."

Hi-Hi stilled himself with long, deep breaths and wagged his head. "Young Josh run so fast."

Hi-Hi pointed to a spot right by his ear. "He kiss me goodbye, and he run "TO." "He run to save little girl."

Phil waited, allowing the tears to soak into the pores of every juror. "Hi-Hi, I am honored, and we are forever in your debt," Phil ended the questioning. "Your Honor, I have no further questions of this witness or about this case."

"Mr. Barstow, do you have any questions of this witness," Clemens offered.

Barstow began filling his briefcase with his files and photographs and statements, which no longer stood a chance of swaying this jury. "No, Your Honor, I can't."

"Does the defense wish to call any more witnesses?" Clemens followed procedure.

"No, Your Honor, the defense rests."

Chapter 25

Judge Clemens called a half-hour recess. He needed the time as much as anyone. Emotion had become the rule of the day. Level heads were required if justice was to be properly served.

Jake and Cassie crammed as many memories as possible into their half-hour with Hi-Hi. Gretchen listened and laughed and cried, "Praise the Lord! AMEN!"

Uncle Phil made a few changes to his closing remarks, now that he knew the whole story. Sarah held Josh's hand while he had a good, long talk with Ben.

The chanting of the multitude outside the courtroom was becoming more and more audible through the windows and the doors.

Judge Clemens called his court back into session with a mighty rap of his gavel as if he wanted Ben to hear. "Is the defense ready to give its closing remarks?"

"Yes, thank you. Your Honor, Ladies, and Gentlemen of the Jury," McCay drawled. "I no longer feel that I need to summarize all the facts in this case. I believe they are emblazoned in your hearts and minds. I leave the decision in your hands, where it should rest. I have only a couple of thoughts to add."

Phil strolled around, with no apparent destination. They were his thoughts that encircled the courtroom, as his hand to his chin demonstrated a pensive state of mind. "The way I see it, Ladies and Gentleman, if I had a little girl or boy missing from my home, I would want Josh and Ben looking for her or him, and I know they would look to the end of their days."

"Did Josh go about the task of finding Melinda Miles in the right way? Detective Hornsby of the Columbus Police Department assured us that Josh was the only man for the job."

"Did a man die at the hands of Josh Marshall? Under Man's law, that cannot be denied. But, under a Higher law, a man died, as all evil does, by his own hand."

"Was it manslaughter that ended the life of a man who did nothing but steal life from a girl who was too young to have hurt anyone? Was it wrongful death that ended a nightmare for a young girl who was ripped from her parents' care? Both premises are unsupportable. And, I must hasten to inform that Josh Marshall is not on trial for either of these charges."

Phil approached the jury head-on. "He is on trial for MURDER!"

Phil receded back to his chair and emphasized, "First-degree murder requires proof of premeditation. I have not seen or heard that proof. The only forethought that has been presented to you is this..."

"Josh devoted himself to the pursuit of a brother's dream. He offered his life for a little girl, who otherwise would not have had a chance. And I ask you, Ladies and Gentlemen, what is to become of us if we lock-up all our heroes? Who will fight for us when the chips are down, and the beast is knocking at our door? Who will watch over our children when we cannot? Who will bring them home when all hope is lost?"

"I shudder to imagine the answers to those questions. But I can tell you what will happen if you acquit Josh Marshall. My darling, Sarah will have a man that all our daughters dream of. A family of over three hundred standing outside this courtroom will go on believing in the country they fought for. Josh will take care of his family with his last ounce of devotion. And I'll wager that Josh will never miss another birthday of Melinda Miles."

McCay took his seat, satisfied that he had done the best he could. He would not win this case. An acquittal would be a victory for Josh and Ben and all those who loved them. Then again, Uncle Phil was one of those who loved him.

"And, Mr. Barstow," Clemens had to ask, "Do you have any closing remarks?"

Barstow had no doubt that the jury would exonerate Josh, but he had a little fence-mending to do. "Yes, your Honor," Barstow acquiescently responded. "I have a few remarks to make to the court and to the jury."

Barstow walked around to the front of his table and leaned back, supporting his exhausted frame against the tabletop, with his hands behind him. "To the court," he humbly submitted, "I would like to report that the prosecution has done it's best to perform its job of protecting and securing our system of justice. We sallied forth, trusting and believing in the evidence at hand. It was never the prosecution's intent to do otherwise."

Barstow approached the jury and offered a more personal note. "It was not my desire to denigrate the defendant's moral character. My goal was not to paint him as a ruthless killer."

Barstow raised his arms high as if pleading for understanding. "But I have to rely on the facts as I see them. They are my stock-in-trade."

Barstow lowered his arms and concluded, "You have been given the facts, and you have heard about the moral character of the defendant. I trust that you will make the right decision. And I trust that justice will be served."

Barstow walked over to the defendant's table and shook the hands of McCay, Sarah, and Josh. "I hope you realize what a lucky young man you are, Mr. Marshall."

"Yes, Sir, I do," Josh respectfully avowed.

Barstow did an about-face and paid his respects to the court. "Your Honor, I request that I be excused from the remainder of these proceedings. I have contributed all I can for the People of the Great State of Texas."

"You are excused," Clemens granted. "And, speaking for the People of the Great State of Texas, the court would like to recognize a job well done."

Barstow paused on his way through the gallery to extend a hand to the father that had believed in his son without question. It was not so much an apology in that gesture of peace, as it was an offer of truce from a man who now believed beyond a shadow of a doubt. Jake accepted that gesture, only to size up the man. There was neither friend nor foe in that handshake. It was a reconciliation between a father who would have given his life for his son, and a man who would give everything to have a son like that.

The jury received its final instructions from Clemens, and they were led out of the courtroom. The fate of justice and mercy lay in their hands. For most of them, this would be the largest decision they had ever had to make.

No one in the gallery left their seat. That would have been equivalent to laying down a gripping novel with only one paragraph to go. This was not only a story of a young man imprisoned for his actions. This was a test of all they believed, and all they held dear. They had followed the footsteps of a young man that embodied all they could dream. They had heard the quest that one selfless soul had proven possible. All the hopes they wished were about to be decided.

The family leaned over the railing and strained to hear. Josh was murmuring every thought that was spilling out of his mind. "I care now. I care what happens to me. It's not just me anymore."

Gretchen laced her fingers together over the railing and rested her chin on her hands. "Ben is right behind you, isn't he Brother?"

"No," Josh differed. "Ben is right beside me. He always has been."

"What is he telling you, Baby?" Cassie beseeched.

Josh cupped his hands over his eyes to block out everything that wasn't Ben. "He's telling me to love. He's telling me to live."

Jake leaned over the rail as far as his brawny frame could reach. "Is he here now, Josh? Is my boy, Ben here?"

Josh turned to meet the eyes of his father, who seldom shed a tear. "He's here, Daddy. As long as I keep breathing, he will be here."

Josh diverted his gaze to Sarah, who was asking for nothing but hoping for everything. "Sarah, if I can – if it turns out that – if there is a chance…"

Sarah wasn't trying to quell Josh's broken words when she put her fingers to his lips. She was trying to feel what she knew he couldn't say.

Phillip McCay was silent through all the impassioned discourse. He knew his presence was only ancillary to the dynamic family drama he overheard. He was only an earwitness to the love that makes a family. That is until he heard Josh say, "Uncle Phil, win or lose, thank you for being my lawyer."

Phil closed his eyes, weighing emotion against pragmatism. He knew what the jury's verdict should be, but he never presumed what it would be. He had seen several cases go from being a sure thing to becoming prey to a jury's subjectively harsh decision. And, he had known many a case that seemed doomed, but inexplicably won the day and secured the future.

Phil dared not meet Josh's eyes. This was not the time to reveal his personal hopes and fears. He laid a hand on Sarah's arm and noticed the beginnings of writer's callous on her middle finger. "Josh, you have already won more than most men will ever know."

Chapter 26

The bailiff sat outside the jury room with his small brown bag. As was his habit, he held a snack and a beverage that would see him through the most protracted deliberation. He had heard testimonies for and against in hundreds of cases, but no one ever asked his opinion. He was under oath not to intervene. His duty was to sit on that hard oak chair and clutch his brown paper bag.

But this case was different from all the rest. This case was about something higher than the common law that governed people's lives. This case was bigger than the decision that twelve people would render. This case was about a young man's hunger and thirst that could not be contained in a brown paper bag.

The brown paper crinkled in the bailiff's clench, as he hoped for the best. His heart was palpitating, and his palms were sweating. The perspiration of worry was beading on his forehead.

He plunged his hand into the paper bag and hurried the can of cold cola to his brow. His breathing was labored, and he didn't know why. Perhaps he didn't realize that his beliefs were also on trial.

He looked at the can that was no longer so cold. It was time to pop the top and wash down the lump residing in his throat. Carbonated gases hissed out of the can, and as the entrapped beverage escaped from the aluminum cylinder, a chorus of roars passed through the jury room door. The effervescent bubbles soaked into the brown paper bag and the clamor of the jury calmed down.

The bailiff stood and smiled. No, it wasn't really a smile, it was a laugh, from deep down inside, that filled his body from head to toe.

The jury was called back to announce its findings. The bailiff placed his brown paper bag and his full can of cola under the chair. He had a parade to lead.

The jurors were lead to their twelve chairs, and the bailiff resumed his post. Judge Clemens entered his court, and all stood at the bailiff's victorious command, "All Rise."

"Has the jury reached a verdict," Judge Clemens officiated.

"Yes, Your Honor, we have," the jury foreman obediently professed. He stood and relished his opportunity to tell a story in his slow, Texas drawl.

"We the Jury find the defendant..."

Scores of lungs were filled with air they could not release. Only the bailiff was breathing easy.

The jury foreman counted to ten in his head and then announced, "We find the defendant guilty of loving."

The mutual exhale could be felt on everyone's cheeks and the back of their heads. The next anxious inhale could be heard as the jury foreman continued.

"We find him guilty of caring."

There were no more breaths held that day. All hearts were freed from their worried distress.

"We find him guilty of unwavering courage and devotion," the foreman humbly, yet proudly declared.

"But, as to the charge of murder?" Judge Clemens had to demand.

The jury foreman gave that ear-to-ear Texas grin. "We the Jury find the defendant – NOT GUILTY!"

That decree soared all the way to Heaven. Surely, Ben could hear. That absolution freed all the hearts that had been locked in anticipation and dread. No seat in the courtroom remained occupied. No voice was silenced by the banging of Clemens' gavel.

The tumult permeated through the doors and spilled out onto the lawn. Over three hundred voices joined the fracas. Kisses of jubilation were exchanged, and hugs of alleviation slowly settled the crowd within and without.

The Honorable Judge Clemens stood to his full stature and raised his gavel high. The unruly throng paused in their celebration to hear that long-awaited proclamation. "The defendant is free to go. He is free to love. He is free to enjoy all the love he deserves."

Clemens lowered the hammer with all the weight of the law. It was as if he was at the county fair with a huge mallet in his hand. He was going to ring the bell for justice with his mighty swing.

The handle of the gavel snapped, and all judgment was severed. The head of the gavel skittered across the floor and months of anguish came to an end at the feet of Josh Marshall.

Josh leaned over to pick up that varnished scepter of justification and held it high. He could see Ben's goofy grin in his mind's eye.

The family rushed in, and Cassie claimed the first hug. "Come straight home. Do you hear me, my Boy?"

"I will, Momma," Josh promised. "Just keep the kitchen light on for me."

Jake clamped his hand in Josh's and gave that fatherly embrace that Josh could not escape. "You do remember the way home, don't you, Son."

"I do, Daddy. I've never forgotten."

Josh placed his hand on Gretchen's head. She was knelt in prayer. There was Someone who needed to be thanked.

Mr. and Mrs. Miles were ready to take their daughter home and close the darkest chapter in their lives. But Melinda was not ready to part ways with her heroes that would never die. She sprang into Josh's arms and committed him to an oath. "When you talk to Ben, tell him that I'm going to be a ballerina. Tell him to watch me fly!"

"Oh, Punkin," Josh swore, "we will both be watching you."

Hi-Hi did not approach. He disappeared as he always had. He had seen all he needed to see. A young man had run "to," and he ambled "away."

Sarah took Josh by the hand and tugged in the direction of the door. It was not the back door of chains and shackles. It was the front door to freedom and the future.

Uncle Phil watched his favorite part of his job. The family marched out of the courtroom without a sliver of light between them.

But Jake did not forget to include one more member of the family. He walked back to shake the hand of the man he had trusted. "Thank you, Phil, for taking care of my boy."

Uncle Phil welcomed the handshake of a brother who had raised the young man he most honored. He didn't join the throng of celebrants and well-wishers. He led the way. He was the first to step into the afternoon light outside the courtroom doors. He didn't shy from the microphones thrust at his face.

He snatched the microphone from the reporter's hand and gave his victorious account. "Justice has been done, and the world is better for it."

The mob that had assembled throughout the day exploded in an unbridled display. Phil waited for the frenzy to subside before he delivered his closing remark. "I give you back your champion and my hero, Mr. Josh Marshall."

The crowd parted at the top of the courthouse steps, and the family emerged into that deafening pandemonium. There was no hope of speaking over the roar, but the multitude didn't need words. All they needed was to see the family reunited arm-in-arm.

A Channel 5 microphone barged in front of Josh's face, in hopes of capturing just a few words. Josh leaned toward the microphone and boomed, "HEY, GUYS, THIS IS SARAH!"

The horde of voices escalated into a joyous, boisterous welcome and Sarah knew that she was now part of that rowdy, unconstrained family.

Josh picked Sarah up in his arms and smacked his lips against hers. He carried her down the steps, and Sarah was high-fiving in every direction. Each hand she touched was a new friend. Each cheer was her welcome reception.

Josh and Sarah were swarmed and ensnared in a sea of love, and there was no escape. But, after all, once they were home, where else would they want to go.

Above the roar that filled their ears, Josh heard a gentle chuckle. It was a voice that could pierce through any shout or scream with its sweet softness.

"Josh?"

Josh spun around and around and searched the crowd. Sarah hung on to his neck and looked with him.

"Josh?"

Josh faced the sun with his eyes clamped shut. It wasn't the glow of the sun that illuminated Josh's face. It was the glow of Ben.

"Yeah, Ben?"

A hush overtook the gang of friends. They could feel, but they could not see. Josh could see, and only Josh could hear.

"Kiss her lots of times, Josh."

Josh laughed in unsurpassable bliss that jostled Sarah in his arms.

"You know I will, Ben."

Josh gave Sarah three quick kisses, and she returned one long, binding kiss.

"Josh?"

Josh remained captive in Sarah's eyes.

"Yeah, Ben?"

Josh listened, and Sarah waited to hear. But all Josh had to give was a tear streaming down his cheek.

Sarah kissed that tear and all its salty affection. "What did Ben say, Sweetheart?"

Josh's smile was more in the corner of his twinkling eye than it was in the curl of his lips. "Ben wants to know if he's going to be an uncle."

Sarah threw her head back and let her hair flow in the breeze. She threw a kiss toward Heaven and answered, "We'll just have to see Brother Ben."

Josh lowered Sarah, so she could stand by his side. It was time for that walk in the park.

"Josh?"

"Hey, Ben, I've gotta go now. I'll catch you later."

"Oh, ok, Josh. You go on ahead."

The human wave made way for Josh and Sarah's stroll. They walked in the silence that love inspires. Only the two of them were on this journey. Only the two of them were in this moment. Except...

"Josh?"

"Yeah, Ben?"

Note from the Author

Word-of-mouth is crucial for any author to succeed. If you enjoyed the book, please leave a review online—anywhere you are able. Even if it's just a sentence or two. It would make all the difference and would be very much appreciated.

Thanks!
Larry

About the Author

Larry W. Plummer's life began on a Kansas farm, where he learned the meaning of family. He earned two college degrees and served in the United State Army Airborne Rangers. He learned how to kill, but he never forgot how to love. Plummer met the love of his life in a piano bar in Monterey, California. That love will never die, and no love story could surpass. His legacy will be two children and four gorgeous grandchildren.

Thank you so much for reading one of our **Larry Plummer's** novels.

If you enjoyed this book, please check out our recommended title for your next great read!

He Never Forgot How to Love by Larry Plummer

Jake escapes his horrific captivity as a prisoner of war in Vietnam. Cassie is a caregiver at the military hospital and nurses Jake back to health. Their love begins over a bowl of Jell-O and carries them back home to the Kansas farm.

Everywhere life takes them, there are others with the same haunting dreams of war. Some have only one leg and some have none. Some have just lost their way home. Cassie and Jake begin with one person at a time and over 27 years, hundreds of vets find a little peace on the bank of the farm pond, and they learn to reach back and help another buddy up the hill.

The best and the worst of us live in these pages and the depth of Jake and Cassie's love can be understood only in the context of the world they dared to change.

View other Black Rose Writing titles at
www.blackrosewriting.com/books and use promo code
PRINT to receive a **20% discount** when purchasing.